Ginsberg   Philip Roth   RENÉ DESCARTES   Theodore
Edna O'Brien   James Me   ami
Philip Larkin   WILLIAM TREVO   V. S.
. Fisher   Fyodor Dostoevsky   JOHN CHEEVER   Joan
M   Margaret Atwood   Franz Kafka   Katherine Anne
n   Julio Cortázar   AMBROSE BIERCE   Helen Keller
.B. Priestley   Gabriel García Márquez   Jorge Luis Borges
sberg   PHILIP ROTH   René Descartes   Theodore Roethke
eish   Edna O'Brien   James Merrill   HARUKI MURAKAMI
rkin   William Trevor   Reynolds Price   V. S. Naipaul
ODOR DOSTOEVSKY   John Cheever   Joan Didion
rgaret Atwood   Franz Kafka   KATHERINE ANNE PORTER
rtázar   Ambrose Bierce   HELEN KELLER   John Updike
iel García Márquez   Jorge Luis Borges   Donald
ip Roth   RENÉ DESCARTES   Theodore Roethke   D. M.
rien   James Merrill   Haruki Murakami   OCTAVIO PAZ
AM TREVOR   Reynolds Price   V. S. Naipaul   Doris
r Dostoevsky   JOHN CHEEVER   Joan Didion   Graham
Franz Kafka   Katherine Anne Porter   VIRGINIA WOOLF
MBROSE BIERCE   Helen Keller   John Updike   Ingmar
García Márquez   Jorge Luis Borges   DONALD BARTHELME
René Descartes   Theodore Roethke   D. M. Thomas
s Merrill   HARUKI MURAKAMI   Octavio Paz
iam Trevor   Reynolds Price   V. S. Naipaul   DORIS
DOR DOSTOEVSKY   John Cheever   Joan Didion   Graham
ood   Franz Kafka   KATHERINE ANNE PORTER   Virginia
ar   Ambrose Bierce   HELEN KELLER   John Updike
l García Márquez   Jorge Luis Borges   Donald Barthelm
RENÉ DESCARTES   Theodore Roethke   D. M
rien   James Merrill   Haruki Murakami   OCTAVIO PAZ
AM TREVOR   Reynolds Price   V. S. Naipaul   Dori
stoevsky   JOHN CHEEVER   Joan Didion   Graham
Franz Kafka   Katherine Anne Porter   VIRGINIA WOOL
r   AMBROSE BIERCE   Helen Keller   John Updik
García Márquez   Jorge Luis Borges   DONALD BARTHELM
TH   René Descartes   Theodore Roethke   D. M. Thoma
es Merrill   HARUKI MURAKAMI   Octavio Paz   Katherin

IN THE HOUSE OF NIGHT

IN THE

House

OF

*N*IGHT

A DREAM READER

∽

EDITED BY
CHRISTOPHER NAVRATIL

CHRONICLE BOOKS
SAN FRANCISCO

ISBN 0-8118-1762-8

Library of Congress Cataloging-in-Publication Data available.

Book and cover design: Pamela Geismar
Composition: Candace Creasy, Blue Friday Type & Graphics
Cover illustration: *Puppets* by Peter Malone from *The Secret Language of Dreams/Dreams Notecards.* © 1994 by Duncan Baird Publishers, Ltd. Reprinted by permission of Duncan Baird Publishers, Ltd.

Printed in the United States of America.

Distributed in Canada by Raincoast Books
8680 Cambie Street
Vancouver, B.C. V6P 6M9

10 9 8 7 6 5 4 3 2 1

Chronicle Books
85 Second Street
San Francisco, CA 94105

Web Site: www.chronbooks.com

CONTENTS

☙

INSPIRATION AND GRATIFICATION

৩৬

✖

Special thanks to
Steve Anderson,
Annie Barrows,
Pamela Geismar,
and
Karen Silver

INTRODUCTION

I am intrigued by the relation of dreams to the dreamer's everyday reality. What do the strange visions manifested in our sleep have to do with the day-to-day functions that make up our life? If they are fabricated from such ordinary threads, why are they often so surreal, and yet occasionally so hyperreal? Frequently I wake up with the sensation of having just returned from a journey of sorts. Some small drama has been acted out in a place that is completely foreign to me, even though it seemed as familiar in my dream world as my encounters with the various strangers there. My dreams are complex. They are sometimes exhilarating, sometimes tranquil, sometimes deeply disturbing or even frightening; but they never cease to fascinate me. As I have grown older, my dreams have become even richer and more vividly detailed; my past and present often intermingle.

A few years ago, I was confronted by a sudden experience of loss. My parents, stricken with different forms of cancer, passed away within a month of each other. Beyond the inevitable grief, I have been struck by how dramatically this event shaped my dreams. These dreams about my parents reflect our entire history together, and the dynamics of our relationship are served up for a closer observation than I had ever considered while my parents were still living. In one dream, I am fifteen again, while they, no longer the enfeebled beings of their later years, are transformed into the more commanding figures of my past, and reconsidered as if I were still living in that past are the long-forgotten issues between

⚜

those parents and that teenager. In a different dream, I am the individual that I perceive myself to be today and in communication with one of them relating the most urgent facts. They are both younger and older, and infinitely wiser, than I had ever imagined them to be. The communication in itself is a kind of revelation. And yet, from these brief moments, it is their profound presence that stays with me. In these dreams they are here once again, as if they had never gone away.

Upon awaking, if alert enough and compelled, I try to capture the essence of a dream, whatever dream. I run through what there is of a narrative structure from the beginning, or the moment of initial realization, to whatever conclusion is reached before waking. I can then hold on to the dream, implant it in my memory for future scrutiny. Later in the day, I will still be able to call it up. I seldom write dreams down. In the few instances that I have, little imagination or "art" on my part has been applied to this function. Instead, by my simple act of recollection, the dream becomes an exercise that I work through for the next few days and then discard. So many dreams, so little time.

A deep interest in my own dreams has led me to an extensive study of the subject. Even though I make limited use of my dreams in my own writing, I am in awe of what a more seasoned writer can make of them. Consider, for example, William Trevor's mesmerizing dream sequence in his novel *Felicia's Journey,* included in this collection. What a startlingly realistic dream Trevor creates. This sequence speaks in the tangled language of dreams, yet a reader can draw from it many of the themes that have been developed on a broader level throughout the entire novel. My appreciation for this kind of writing has been my inspiration for assembling this anthology. I am dazzled by a writer's ability to capture, through a descriptive ordering of images and symbols, the ephemeral quality of a dream while at the same time creating a compelling narrative in fiction, poetry, or prose.

With a few exceptions, the pieces included in *In the House of Night* focus on twentieth-century writers. My feeling is that, prior to the late nineteenth century, few writers approached the subject of dreams from an analytical basis. There are, of course, examples of dream writing that go back to the ancient Greeks, and dreams are present in the writings of Chaucer and Shakespeare. But whether their own dreams were the source of this material or they merely saw in the subject a convenient tool or plot device is a subject for more extensive literary research. It took the writings of Freud and Jung, in the early years of the twentieth century, to get the whole preoccupation with dreams securely underway, and with it, a more introspective approach to the realm of dreams. For one thing, many writers began to record their own dreams. In some cases, these dream entries exist for the reader today simply as reflections of these writers' inner lives, but occasionally you can find signposts there for their more developed work to come later. Could you imagine the impact if one were to unearth a dream diary by Shakespeare, or perhaps even Jane Austen? A light would be shed on their lives and work that would dramatically alter all previous scholarship done on these authors.

Dreams and analysis naturally go hand in hand. The journals of writers as diverse as Edmund Wilson, Katherine Mansfield, Franz Kafka, and C. S. Lewis are loaded with dreams. Graham Greene went even further, keeping a separate journal in which to record his dreams. In reading through some of these dreams today, we can't help but read them for what they tell us about the psychology of the writer. In some, the dreams merely confirm our suspicions, but there are some curiosities. It probably isn't astonishing that Edmund Wilson's obsessive nature would so often poke through in his dreams, but I find it interesting that he would have recurrent dreams about his second wife twenty years and two wives after her death. Better yet, who could have imagined that Graham Greene, a master of intrigue and suspense, would keep a detailed record of the dreams in which he had conversations with various dogs?

In doing research for this book, I have discovered that, in relation to dreams, writers tend to fall into two categories: those who are intensely interested in the subject and who choose to incorporate dreams into their work, and those who are indifferent. The writers in the first category offer up a rich selection of dreams to choose from. Doris Lessing and Margaret Atwood, for instance, have written extensively and imaginatively on the subject in their fiction. Since their writing so vividly explores the subject, I assume that they have had rich dream lives on which to draw.

Also included within the first group are those writers who not only have chosen to write about their own dreams but who pay tribute to the subject. The essays by Jean Cocteau and J. B. Priestley directly reveal how dreams have enriched their lives. Priestley claims that "As a child I could never understand why grown-ups took dreaming so calmly when they could make such a fuss about any holiday." Similarly, poems by John Updike and Elizabeth Bishop pay homage to the more ephemeral qualities that dreams embody; each is entranced by dreams' physical dimensions. He is struck by "their three-dimensional workmanship." She refers to them as "armored cars . . . all camouflaged, and ready to go through the swiftest streams."

The second category, as you might imagine, presents a few more difficulties. Take, for example, May Sarton, whose work I have chosen not to include in this book. There are a few brief dream passages scattered throughout her numerous journals, but for the most part she devotes very little time to them. Given that her prose lends itself so well to introspective analysis, I expected that she would draw more from dreams. In one of her later journals, *Recovering*, Sarton discusses her prior aversion to the subject: "I used to be bored by dreams, my own or those of others, not inclined to pay attention to them as valid signposts or alerts, but Karen Buss sent me *The Dream Makers*, a book about breakthrough dreaming by two psychiatrists. I read it on Sark and found it convincing. No doubt what is buried tries to make its way through in dreams."

Another example is John Cheever. A dream is a rare find in either his fiction or his journals. The few examples, however, are so deliciously fascinating (and neurotic) that I can't help but be disappointed that he didn't write more extensively on the subject. And then there's Philip Roth, whom I place in this second category as well. The sequence from *Portnoy's Complaint* included in this book is in fact a kind of anti-dream, a tease in a way. Roth has many of the familiar elements in place, and he knows the significance of dream symbols; but ultimately he has created a reality sequence, an angst-ridden journey to Israel disguised beneath a surreal stream of dream-like prose.

Through a selection of approximately fifty pieces ranging from poetry and fiction to diary excerpts and essays, *In the House of Night* attempts to portray dreams as a medium for providing creative insight into the inner workings of an individual's life, both in reality and in fiction. The selections are arranged in seven loosely themed chapters that are intended to inspire the reader's individual interpretation. All dreams are loaded with significant imagery, and any one dream could have a number of different meanings. Rather than attempt to slot these pieces into narrowly defined categories, I instead offer the reader, through the sequence of chapters, some broad themes to consider. The sections are titled Asleep and Awake, Desire and Love, Sorrow and Remorse, Identity and Discovery, Anxiety and Neurosis, Death and Escape, and Inspiration and Gratification. The pieces included in each section present alternate perspectives on these subjects. Although the chapters are loosely themed, these pieces have been selected and organized with the cumulative effect of the entire collection in mind. My aim has been to create a stimulating and entertaining anthology that, ultimately, will satisfy a taste for the artistic mastery of accomplished dream writing and, perhaps, encourage further investigation into the reader's own dreams.

ASLEEP AND AWAKE

D O N A L D   B A R T H E L M E

✖

“A FEW MOMENTS OF

SLEEPING AND WAKING”

An original and much-imitated American novelist and short-story writer, Donald Barthelme's (1931–1989) distinctively fragmented prose would often employ pop cultural clichés and media jargon. His novels include *Snow White* and *The Dead Father.* A frequent contributor of short fiction to *The New Yorker* magazine, his collected works include *Sixty Stories, Overnight to Many Distant Cities,* and *Forty Stories,* from which this story was taken.

*E*dward woke up. Pia was already awake.

"What did you dream?"

"You were my brother," Pia said. "We were making a film. You were the hero. It was a costume film. You had a cape and a sword. You were jumping about, jumping on tables. But in the second half of the film you had lost all your weight. You were thin. The film was ruined. The parts didn't match."

"I was your brother?"

Scarlatti from the radio. It was Sunday. Pete sat at the breakfast table. Pete was a doctor on an American nuclear submarine, a psychiatrist. He had just come off patrol, fifty-eight days under the water. Pia gave Pete scrambled eggs with mushrooms, *wienerbrød,* salami with red wine in it, bacon. Pete interpreted Pia's dream.

"Edward was your brother?"

"Yes."

"And your real brother is going to Italy, you said."

"Yes."

"It may be something as simple as a desire to travel."

Edward and Pia and Pete went for a boat ride, a tour of the Copenhagen harbor. The boat held one hundred and twenty tourists. They sat, four tourists abreast, on either side of the aisle. A guide spoke into a microphone in Danish, French, German, and English, telling the tourists what was in the harbor.

"I interpreted that dream very sketchily," Pete said to Edward.

"Yes."

"I could have done a lot more with it."

"Don't."

"This is the Danish submarine fleet," the guide said into the microphone. Edward and Pia and Pete regarded the four black submarines. There had been a flick every night on Pete's submarine. Pete discussed the fifty-eight flicks he had seen. Pete sat on Edward's couch discussing *The Sound of Music*. Edward made drinks. Rose's Lime Juice fell into the gimlet glasses. Then Edward and Pia took Pete to the airport. Pete flew away. Edward bought *The Interpretation of Dreams*.

Pia dreamed that she had journeyed to a great house, a castle, to sing. She had found herself a bed in a room overlooking elaborate gardens. Then another girl appeared, a childhood friend. The new girl demanded Pia's bed. Pia refused. The other girl insisted. Pia refused. The other girl began to sing. She sang horribly. Pia asked her to stop. Other singers appeared, demanding that Pia surrender the bed. Pia refused. People stood about the bed, shouting and singing.

Edward smoked a cigar. "Why didn't you just give her the bed?"

"My honor would be hurt," Pia said. "You know, that girl is not like that. Really she is very quiet and not asserting—

⚓

asserting?—asserting herself. My mother said I should be more like her."

"The dream was saying that your mother was wrong about this girl?"

"Perhaps."

"What else?"

"I can't remember."

"Did you sing?"

"I can't remember," Pia said.

Pia's brother Søren rang the doorbell. He was carrying a pair of trousers. Pia sewed up a split in the seat. Edward made instant coffee. Pia explained *blufaerdighedskraenkelse.* "If you walk with your trousers open," she said. Søren gave Edward and Pia *The Joan Baez Songbook.* "It is a very good one," he said in English. The doorbell rang. It was Pia's father. He was carrying a pair of shoes Pia had left at the farm. Edward made more coffee. Pia sat on the floor cutting a dress out of blue, red, and green cloth. Ole arrived. He was carrying his guitar. He began to play something from *The Joan Baez Songbook.* Edward regarded Ole's Mowgli hair. We be of one blood, thee and I. Edward read *The Interpretation of Dreams.* "In cases where not my ego but only a strange person appears in the dream-content, I may safely assume that by means of identification my ego is concealed behind that person. I am permitted to supplement my ego."

Edward sat at a sidewalk café drinking a beer. He was wearing his brown suède shoes, his black dungarees, his black-and-white-checked shirt, his red beard, his immense spectacles. Edward regarded his hands. His hands seemed old. "I am thirty-three." Tiny girls walked past the sidewalk café wearing skintight black pants. Then large girls in skintight white pants.

Edward and Pia walked along Frederiksberg Allé, under the queer box-cut trees. "Here I was knocked off my bicycle when I was seven," Pia said. "By a car. In a snowstorm."

Edward regarded the famous intersection. "Were you hurt?"

"My bicycle was demolished utterly."

Edward read *The Interpretation of Dreams*. Pia bent over the sewing machine, sewing blue, red, and green cloth.

"Freud turned his friend R. into a disreputable uncle, in a dream."

"Why?"

"He wanted to be an assistant professor. He was bucking for assistant professor."

"So why was it not allowed?"

"They didn't know he was Freud. They hadn't seen the movie."

"You're joking."

"I'm trying."

Edward and Pia talked about dreams. Pia said she had been dreaming about unhappy love affairs. In these dreams, she said, she was very unhappy. Then she woke, relieved.

"How long?"

"For about two months, I think. But then I wake up and I'm happy. That it is not so."

"Why are they *unhappy* love affairs?"

"I don't know."

"Do you think it means you want new love affairs?"

"Why should I want unhappy love affairs?"

"Maybe you want to have love affairs but feel guilty about wanting to have love affairs, and so they become unhappy love affairs."

"That's subtle," Pia said. "You're insecure."

"Ho!" Edward said.

"But why then am I happy when I wake up?"

"Because you don't have to feel guilty anymore," Edward said glibly.

"Ho!" Pia said.

Edward resisted *The Interpretation of Dreams*. He read eight novels by Anthony Powell. Pia walked down the street in Edward's blue sweater. She looked at herself in a shop window. Her hair was rotten. Pia went into the bathroom and played with her hair for one hour. Then she brushed her teeth for a bit. Her hair was still rotten. Pia sat down and began to cry. She cried for a quarter hour, without making any noise. Everything was rotten.

Edward bought *Madam Cherokee's Dream Book*. Dreams in alphabetical order. If you dream of black cloth, there will be a death in the family. If you dream of scissors, a birth. Edward and Pia saw three films by Jean-Luc Godard. The landlord came and asked Edward to pay Danish income tax. "But I don't make any money in Denmark," Edward said. Everything was rotten.

Pia came home from the hairdresser with black varnish around her eyes.

"How do you like it?"

"I hate it."

Pia was chopping up an enormous cabbage, a cabbage big as a basketball. The cabbage was of an extraordinary size. It was a big cabbage.

"That's a big cabbage," Edward said.

"Big," Pia said.

They regarded the enormous cabbage God had placed in the world for supper.

"Is there vinegar?" Edward asked. "I like . . . vinegar . . . with my . . ." Edward read a magazine for men full of colored photographs of naked girls living normal lives. Edward read the *New Statesman,* with its letters to the editor. Pia appeared in her new blue, red, and green dress. She looked wonderful.

"You look wonderful."

"*Tak.*"

"Tables are women," Edward said. "You remember you said I was jumping on tables, in your dream. Freud says that tables are figures for women. You're insecure."

"*La vache!*" Pia said.

Pia reported a new dream. "I came home to a small town where I was born. First, I ran around as a tourist with my camera. Then a boy who was selling something—from one of those little wagons?—asked me to take his picture. But I couldn't find him in the photo *apparat.* In the view glass. Always other people got in the way. Everyone in this town was divorced. Everybody I knew. Then I went to a ladies' club, a place where the women asked the men to dance. But there was only one man there. His picture was on an advertisement outside. He was the gigolo. Gigolo? Is that right? Then I called up people I knew, on the telephone. But they were all divorced. Everybody was divorced. My mother and father were divorced. Helle and Jens were divorced. Everybody. Everybody was floating about in a strange way."

Edward groaned. A palpable groan. "What else?"

"I can't remember."

"Nothing else?"

"When I was on my way to the ladies' club, the boy I had tried to take a picture of came up and took my arm. I was surprised but I said to myself something like, *It's necessary to have friends here.*"

"What else?"

"I can't remember."

"Did you sleep with him?"

"I don't remember."

"What did the ladies' club remind you of?"

"It was in a cellar."

"Did it remind you of anything?"

"It was rather like a place at the university. Where we used to dance."

"What is connected with that place in your mind?"

"Once a boy came through a window to a party."

"Why did he come through the window?"

"So he didn't pay."

"Who was he?"

"Someone."

"Did you dance with him?"

"Yes."

"Did you sleep with him?"

"Yes."

"Very often?"

"Twice."

Edward and Pia went to Malmö on the flying boat. The hydrofoil leaped into the air. The feeling was that of a plane laboring down an interminable runway.

"I dreamed of a roof," Pia said. "Where corn was kept. Where it was stored."

"What does that—" Edward began.

"Also I dreamed of rugs. I was beating a rug," she went on. "And I dreamed about horses, I was riding."

"Don't," Edward said.

Pia silently rehearsed three additional dreams. Edward regarded the green leaves of Malmö. Edward and Pia moved through the rug department of a department store. Surrounded by exciting rugs: Rya rugs, Polish rugs, rag rugs, straw rugs, area rugs, wall-to-wall rugs, rug remnants.

✿

Edward was thinking about one that cost five hundred crowns, in seven shades of red, about the size of an opened-up *Herald Tribune*, Paris edition.

"It is too good for the floor, clearly," Pia said. "It is to be hung on the wall."

Edward had four hundred dollars in his pocket. It was supposed to last him two months. The hideously smiling rug salesman pressed closer. They burst into the street. Just in time. "God knows they're beautiful, however," Edward said.

"What did you dream last night?" Edward asked. "What did you dream? What?"

"I can't remember."

Edward decided that he worried too much about the dark side of Pia. Pia regarded as a moon. Edward lay in bed trying to remember a dream. He could not remember. It was eight o'clock. Edward climbed out of bed to see if there was mail on the floor, if mail had fallen through the door. No. Pia awoke.

"I dreamed of beans."

Edward looked at her. *Madam Cherokee's Dream Book* flew into his hand.

"The dream of beans is, in all cases, very unfortunate. Eating them means sickness, preparing them means that the married state will be a very difficult one for you. To dream of *beets* is on the other hand a happy omen."

Edward and Pia argued about *Mrs. Miniver*. It was not written by J. B. Priestley, Edward said.

"I remember it very well," Pia insisted. "Errol Flynn was her husband, he was standing there with his straps, his straps" —Pia made a holding-up-trousers gesture—"hanging, and she said that she loved Walter Pidgeon."

"Errol Flynn was not even in the picture. You think J. B. Priestley wrote everything, don't you? Everything in English."

"I don't."

"Errol Flynn was not even in the picture." Edward was drunk. He was shouting. "Errol Flynn was not even . . . *in* . . . the goddamn *picture!*"

Pia was not quite asleep. She was standing on a street corner. Women regarded her out of the corners of their eyes. She was holding a string bag containing strawberries, beer, razor blades, turnips. An old lady rode up on a bicycle and stopped for the traffic light. The old lady straddled her bicycle, seized Pia's string bag, and threw it into the gutter. Then she pedaled away, with the changing light. People crowded around. Someone picked up the string bag. Pia shook her head. "No," she said. "She just . . . I have never seen her before." Someone asked Pia if she wanted him to call a policeman. "What for?" Pia said. Her father was standing there smiling. Pia thought, *These things have no significance really.* Pia thought, *If this is to be my dream for tonight, then I don't want it.*

STANLEY   ELKIN

❧

from M R S .   T E D   B L I S S

Known for bringing an absurdist, dark-humored vision to highly
realistic portraits of American life, Stanley Elkin's (1930–1995)
novels include *The Dick Gibson Show, George Mills,* and *The Magic
Kingdom.* In this late sequence from *Mrs. Ted Bliss,* the central
character, an elderly widow who has been living in a slowly deteri-
orating condominium complex in Miami for the past twenty-five
years, is left alone in her apartment to face the consequences of an
impending hurricane. Having survived her share of disappoint-
ments, Mrs. Bliss emerges at this point in the novel wiser and
more self-assured. Anticipating the storm's arrival, the novel's
culminating event, she drifts in and out of her dreams with a sense
of tranquil resolution.

*I*n her dreams the hurricane was even
more animated than it was in actuality. She got better reception in her dreams. For one thing it was already light out. She
couldn't judge what time it was but supposed early morning
since she saw no sun. Of course that might have been an illusion created by the gloom—some mean average by-product
of the practically biblical rain. So God knows when those first
few palm trees flew past her seventh-story balcony. It could
have been as early as seven or as late as half-past six in the
afternoon. Whatever the time, this was the worst Mrs. Bliss
had seen yet. The trees flew past so rapidly and on so horizontal a course they could have been wooden torpedoes.
She'd have risen from the wing chair, walked to the drapes to

shut them to protect herself from the constant necessity of blinking or throwing up her hands like a boxer trying to protect his head if it hadn't been for her fear that at any moment the wind could shift, *pfftt, bam,* just like that, and drive one of those palms directly through the sliding glass doors. There was nothing more Mrs. Bliss could do. Tracking the hurricane was fatuous now, quantifying it was. She dreamed she had fallen asleep in her chair, she dreamed that the eye of the hurricane had already passed over.

With this, she dreamed of how very depressed she was, for if its eye had passed over, then not only was the worst yet to come (and hadn't it—those palm trees whizzing past— already started?) but she had missed out on what was said to be the most exhilarating aspect of a hurricane—the intense feeling of well-being and soft, luxurious fatigue that accompanied an extended period of low pressure. The experts were all agreed on this part, hammering away at their theme, their own disclaimer. You must steel yourself against the soft seduction of the eye's low pressure, its perfect dust- and pollen-raked sweet room temperature ionized air, as though the same powerful winds that had blown it over and around her had pushed away all shmuts before them like a new beginning of the world. Stay indoors, stay indoors, they warned, drilling its dangers at her like a public service announcement. You couldn't have paid her, who'd missed so much, to miss this.

And now she had, and woke from her unplanned sleep with a fatigue as sour as a hangover.

Confused, disoriented, she saw that it was still dark but took no comfort from the fact that she had not missed the eye's wondrous performance.

"ON DREAMS"

Jean Cocteau (1889–1963), a French poet, novelist, dramatist, essayist, and filmmaker, was at the forefront of almost every experimental artistic movement in the first half of the twentieth century. His poetic novels include *The Imposter* and *Les Enfants terribles,* which he eventually brought to the screen in 1950. Cocteau is probably best known to American audiences for his lushly poetic adaptation of *Beauty and the Beast* in 1945.

A session at Dr B's, with nitrogen protoxyde comes to my mind. The nurse is giving this to me. The door opens. Another nurse comes in and says the word *Madame.* I leave our world, not without believing that I am countering the gas with a superior lucidity. I even seem to have the strength to make some very subtle remarks. 'Doctor, take care, I am not asleep.' But the journey begins. It lasts for centuries. I reach the first tribunal. I am judged. I pass. Another century. I reach the second tribunal. I am judged. I pass and so it continues. At the fourteenth tribunal I understand that multiplicity is the sign of this other world and unity the sign of ours. I shall find on return one body, one dentist, one dentist's room, one dentist's hand, one dentist's lamp, one dentist's chair, one dentist's white coat. And soon I must forget what I have seen. Retrace my steps before all these tribunals. Realize that they know that it is of no importance, that I shall not talk about it because I shall not remember. Centuries are added to centuries. I re-enter our

world. I see unity reforming. What a bore! Everything is one.
And I hear a voice saying at the door: '. . . wishes to know if
you will see her tomorrow.' The nurse is finishing her sentence. Only the name of the lady has escaped me. This is the
duration of the centuries from which I'm surfacing, this
the expanse of my dizzy journey. It is the immediacy of the
dream. All we remember is the interminable dream that
occurs instantaneously on the brink of awakening. I have
said that my dreams were usually of the nature of caricatures.
They accuse me. They inform me of what is irreparable in my
nature. They underline organic imperfections I will not cor-
rect. I suspected these. The dream proves them to me by means
of acts, apologues, speeches. It is not like this every time,
unless I flatter myself, not having unravelled the meaning.

The swiftness of the dream is such that its scenes are
peopled with objects unknown to us when awake and about
which in a trice we know the minutest details. What strikes
me is that, from one second to the next, our ego of the dream
finds itself projected into a new world, without feeling the
astonishment which this world would rouse in it in a waking
state, although it remains itself and does not participate in
this transfiguration. We ourselves remain in another universe, which might suggest that when falling asleep we are like
a traveller who awakes with a start. Nothing of the kind, since
the town, where he did not believe himself to be, surprises
this traveller, whereas the extravaganzas of a dream never disconcert the waking man who falls asleep. So the dream is the
sleeper's normal existence. This is why I endeavour to forget
my dreams on waking. The actions of a dream are not valid
in a waking state and the actions of the waking state are only
valid in the dream because it has the digestive faculty of making them into excrement. In the world of sleep this excrement
does not appear to us as such and its chemistry interests us,

amuses us or terrifies us. But transposed into the waking
state, which does not possess this digestive faculty, the actions
of the dream would foul life for us and make it unbreathable.
Thousands of examples prove this, because in recent times a
good many doors have been opened to these horrors. It is one
thing to look for signs in them and another to allow the oil
stain to spread over to the waking state and extend there.
Fortunately our neighbour's dream bores us if he recounts it
to us and this fact stops us from recounting our own.

What is certain is that this enfolding, through the
medium of which eternity becomes liveable to us, is not pro-
duced in dreams in the same way as in life. Something of this
fold unfolds. Thanks to this our limits change, widen. The
past, the future no longer exist; the dead rise again; places
construct themselves without architect, without journeys,
without that tedious oppression that compels us to live
minute by minute that which the half-opened fold shows us
at a glance. Moreover the atmospheric and profound trivial-
ity of the dream favours encounters, surprises, acquain-
tanceships, a naturalness, which our enfolded world (I mean
projected on to the surface of a fold) can only ascribe to the
supernatural. I say naturalness, because one of the charac-
teristics of the dream is that nothing in it astonishes us. We
consent without regret to live there among strangers, entirely
separated from our habits and our friends. This is what fills
us with dismay at the sight of a face we love, and which is
asleep. Where, at this moment, stirs the face behind this
mask? Where does it light up and for whom? This sight of
sleep has always frightened me more than dreams. I made the
verses of *Plain-Chant* about it.

A woman sleeps. She triumphs. She need no longer lie.
She is a lie from head to toe. She will give no account of her
movements. She deceives with impunity. Taking advantage of

this licentiousness, she parts her lips, she allows her limbs to drift where they will. She is no longer on guard. She is her own alibi. What could the man watching her blame her for? She is there. What need has Othello of that handkerchief? Let him watch Desdemona sleeping. It is enough to make one commit murder. It is true that a jealous man never ceases to be one and that afterwards he would exclaim: 'What is she doing to me there among the dead?'

Emerged from sleep the dream fades. It is a deep sea plant which dies out of water. It dies on my sheets. Its reign mystifies me. I admire its fables. I take advantage of it to live a double life. I never make use of it.

What it teaches us is the bitterness of our limitations. Since Nerval, Ducasse, Rimbaud, the study of its mechanism has often given the poet the means of conquering them, adapting our world otherwise than according to the dictates of good sense, shuffling the order of the factors to which reason condemns us, in short making for poetry a lighter, swifter and newer vehicle.

ALLEN GINSBERG

⚬

"UNDERSTAND THAT THIS
IS A DREAM"

One of the most prominent American poets to emerge from the Beat
Generation, Allen Ginsberg's (1926–1997) publication of *Howl and
Other Poems* in 1956 marked a revolutionary change in the direction
of American poetry. His spontaneous approach to new and alterna-
tive areas of culture and experience led a departure from the more
rigidly organized poetry written prior to the mid-1950s. The poem
originally appeared in *Reality Sandwiches* in 1963.

*R*eal as a dream
What shall I do with this great opportunity to fly?
What is the interpretation of this planet, this moon?
If I can dream that I dream / and dream anything
      dreamable / can I dream
I am awake / and why do that?
When I dream in a dream that I wake / up what
happens when I try to move?
I dream that I move
and the effort moves and moves
till I move / and my arm hurts
Then I wake up / dismayed / I was dreaming / I was waking
when I was dreaming still / just now.
and try to remember next time in dreams
that I am in dreaming.
And dream anything I want when I'm awaken.

When I'm in awakeness what do I desire?
I desire to fulfill my emotional belly.
My whole body my heart in my fingertips thrill with some
    old fulfillments.
Pages of celestial rhymes burning fire-words
unconsumable but disappear.
Arcane parchments my own and the universe the answer.
Belly to Belly and knee to knee.
The hot spurt of my body to thee to thee
old boy / dreamy Earl / you Prince of Paterson / now king
    of me / lost Haledon
first dream that made me take down my pants
urgently to show the cars / auto trucks / rolling down
    avenue hill.
That far back what do I remember / but the face of the
    leader of the gang
was blond / that loved me / one day on the steps of his
    house blocks away
all afternoon I told him about my magic Spell
I can do anything I want / palaces millions / chemistry
    sets / chicken coops / white horses
stables and torture basements / I inspect my naked victims
chained upside down / my fingertips thrill approval on
    their thighs
white hairless cheeks I may kiss all I want
at my mercy. on the racks.
I pass with my strong attendants / I am myself naked
bending down with my buttocks out
for their smacks of reproval / o the heat of desire
like shit in my asshole. The strange gang
across the street / thru the grocerystore / in the wood alley /
    out in the open on the corner /

Because I lied to the Dentist about that chickencoop
     roofing / slate stolen off his garage
by me and the boy I loved who would punish me if he knew
what I loved him.
That now I have had that boy back in another blond form
Peter Orlovsky a Chinese teenager in Bangkok ten years
     twenty years
Joe Army on the campus / white blond loins / my mouth
     hath kisses /
full of his cock / my ass burning / full of his cock
all that I do desire. In dream and awake
this handsome body mine / answered
all I desired / intimate loves /open eyed / revealed at last /
     clothes on the floor
Underwear the most revealing stripped off below the belly
     button in bed.
That's that / yes yes / the flat cocks the red pricks the gentle
     pubic hair / alone with me
my magic spell. My power / what I desire alone / what after
     thirty years /
I got forever / after thirty years / satisfied enough with
     Peter / with all I wanted /
with many men I knew one generation / our sperm passing
into our mouths and bellies / beautiful when love / given.
Now the dream oldens / I olden / my hair a year long / my
     thirtyeight birthday approaching.
I dream I
am bald / am disappearing / the campus unrecognizable /
     Haledon Avenue
will be covered with neon / motels / Supermarkets / iron
The porches and woods changed when I go back / to see
     Earl again

He'll be a bald / fleshy father / I could pursue him further
    in the garage
If there's still a garage on the hill / on the planet / when
    I get back. From Asia.
If I could even remember his name or his face / or find him /
When I was ten / perhaps he exists in some form.
With a belly and a belt and an auto
Whatever his last name / I never knew / in the phonebook /
    the Akashic records.
I'll write my Inspiration for all Mankind to remember,
My Idea, the secret cave / in the clothes closet / that house
    probably down /
Nothing to go back to / everything's gone / only my idea
That's disappearing / even in dreams / gray dust piles /
    instant annihilation
of World War II and all its stainless steel shining-mouthed
    cannons
much less me and my grammar school kisses / I never
    kissed in time /
and go on kissing in dream and out on the street / as if it
    were for ever.
No forever left! Even my oldest forever gone, in Bangkok, in
    Benares,
swept up with words and bodies / all into the brown
    Ganges /
passing the burning grounds and / into the police state.
My mind, my mind / you had six feet of Earth to hoe /
Why didn't you remember and plant the seed of Law and
    gather the sprouts of What?
the golden blossoms of what idea? If I dream that I dream /
    what dream
should I dream next? Motorcycle rickshaws / parting lamp
    shine / little taxis / horses' hoofs

on this Saigon midnight street. Angkor Wat ahead and the
    ruined city's old Hindu faces
and there was a dream about Eternity. What should I dream
    when I wake?
What's left to dream, more Chinese meat? More magic
    Spells? More youths to love before I change &
    disappear?
More dream words? This can't go on forever. Now that
    I know it all /
goes whither? For now that I know I am dreaming /
What next for you Allen? Run down to the Presidents
    Palace full of Morphine /
the cocks crowing / in the street. / Dawn trucks / What is
    the question?
Do I need sleep, now that there's light in the window?
I'll go to sleep. Signing off until / the next idea / the moving
    van arrives empty
at the Doctor's house full of Chinese furniture.

Saigon, May 31–June 1, 1963

❦

from PORTNOY'S COMPLAINT

Philip Roth, an American novelist and short-story writer, has authored some of the most acclaimed and popular novels of the last few decades. Best known for his irreverent observations of contemporary Jewish-American culture, Roth's critical and popular success, *Goodbye, Columbus,* was followed by novels such as *Letting Go, The Ghost Writer, The Counterlife,* and *Sabbath's Theater.*

*M*y dream begins as soon as I disembark. *I am in an airport where I have never been before and all the people I see—passengers, stewardesses, ticket sellers, porters, pilots, taxi drivers—are Jews.* Is that so unlike the dreams that your dreaming patients recount? Is that so unlike the kind of experience one has while asleep? But awake, who ever heard of such a thing? The writing on the walls is Jewish—Jewish graffiti! The *flag* is Jewish. The faces are the faces you see on Chancellor Avenue! The faces of my neighbors, my uncles, my teachers, the parents of my boyhood friends. Faces like my own face! only moving before a backdrop of white wall and blazing sun and spikey tropical foliage. And it ain't Miami Beach, either. No, the faces of Eastern Europe, but only a stone's throw from Africa! In their short pants the men remind me of the head counselors at the Jewish summer camps I worked at during college vacations—only this isn't summer camp, either. It's home! These aren't Newark high school teachers off for two months with a clipboard and a whistle in the Hopatcong mountains of New Jersey. These are (there's no other word!) the natives. Returned! This is where it all began! Just been away on a long vacation, that's all! Hey, here *we're the WASPs! My taxi passes through a big square surrounded by sidewalk cafés such as one might see in Paris or Rome. Only the cafés are crowded with Jews. The taxi overtakes a bus. I look inside its windows. More Jews. Including the driver. Including the policemen up ahead directing traffic! At the hotel I ask the clerk for a room. He has a thin mustache and speaks English as though he were Ronald Colman. Yet he is Jewish too.*

And now the drama thickens:

It is after midnight. Earlier in the evening, the promenade beside the sea was a gay and lively crush of Jews—Jews eating ices, Jews drinking soda pop, Jews conversing, laughing, walking together arm-in-arm. But now as I start back to my hotel, I find myself virtually alone. At the end of the promenade, which I must pass beyond to reach my hotel, I see five youths smoking cigarettes and talking. Jewish youths, of course. As I approach them, it becomes clear to me that they have been anticipating my arrival. One of them steps forward and addresses me in English. "What time is it?" I look at my watch and realize that they are not going to permit me to pass. They are going to assault me! But how can that be? If they are Jewish and I am Jewish, what motive can there be for them to do me any harm?

I must tell them that they are making a mistake. Surely they do not really want to treat me as a gang of anti-Semites would. "Pardon me," I say, and edge my body between them, wearing a stern expression on my pale face. One of them calls, "Mister, what time—?" whereupon I quicken my pace and continue rapidly to the hotel, unable to understand why they should have wished to frighten me so, when we are all Jews.

Hardly defies interpretation, wouldn't you say?

In my room I quickly remove my trousers and shorts and under a reading lamp examine my penis. I find the organ to be unblemished and without any apparent signs of disease, and yet I am not relieved. It may be that in certain cases (perhaps those that are actually most severe) there is never any outward manifestation of infection. Rather, the debilitating effects take place within the body, unseen and unchecked, until at last the progress of the disorder is irreversible, and the patient is doomed.

In the morning I am awakened by the noise from beyond my window. It is just seven o'clock, yet when I look outside I see the beach already swarming with people. It is a startling sight at such an early hour, particularly as the day is Saturday and I was anticipating a sabbath mood of piety and solemnity to pervade the city. But the crowd of Jews—yet again!—is gay. I examine my member in the strong morning light and am— yet again—overcome with apprehension to discover that it appears to be in a perfectly healthy condition.

I leave my room to go and splash in the sea with the happy Jews. I bathe where the crowd is most dense. I am playing in a sea full of Jews! Frolicking, gamboling Jews! Look at their Jewish limbs moving through the Jewish water! Look at the Jewish children laughing, acting as if they own the place . . . Which they do! And the lifeguard, yet another Jew! Up and down the beach, so far as I can see, Jews—and more pouring in throughout the beautiful morning, as from a cornucopia. I stretch out on the beach, I close my eyes. Overhead I hear an engine: no fear, a Jewish plane. Under me the sand is warm: Jewish sand. I buy a Jewish ice cream from a Jewish vendor. "Isn't this something?" I say to myself. "A Jewish country!" But the idea is more easily expressed than understood; I cannot really grasp hold of it. Alex in Wonderland.

In the afternoon I befriend a young woman with green eyes and tawny skin who is a lieutenant in the Jewish Army. The Lieutenant takes me at night to a bar in the harbor area. The customers, she says, are mostly longshoremen. Jewish

longshoremen? Yes. I laugh, and she asks me what's so funny.
I am excited by her small, voluptuous figure nipped at the
middle by the wide webbing of her khaki belt. But what a deter-
mined humorless self-possessed little thing! I don't know if she
would allow me to order for her even if I spoke the language.
"Which do you like better?" she asks me, after each of us has
downed a bottle of Jewish beer, "tractors, or bulldozers, or
tanks?" I laugh again.

I ask her back to my hotel. In the room we struggle, we
kiss, we begin to undress, and promptly I lose my erection. "See,"
says The Lieutenant, as though confirmed now in her suspicion,
"you don't like me. Not at all." "Yes, oh yes," I answer, "since
I saw you in the sea, I do, I do, you are sleek as a little seal—"
but then, in my shame, baffled and undone by my detumescence,
I burst out—"but I may have a disease, you see. It wouldn't be
fair." "Do you think that is funny too?" she hisses, and angrily
puts her uniform back on and leaves.

Dreams? If only they had been! But I don't need dreams,
Doctor, that's why I hardly have them—because I have this
life instead. With me it all happens in broad daylight! The dis-
proportionate and the melodramatic, this is my daily bread!
The coincidences of dreams, the symbols, the terrifyingly
laughable situations, the oddly ominous banalities, the acci-
dents and humiliations, the bizarrely appropriate strokes of
luck or misfortune that other people experience with their
eyes shut, I get with mine open! Who else do you know whose
mother actually threatened him with the dreaded knife?
Who else was so lucky as to have the threat of castration so
straight-forwardly put by his momma? Who else, on top of
this mother, had a testicle that wouldn't descend? A nut that
had to be coaxed and coddled, *persuaded,* drugged! to get it
to come down and live in the scrotum like a man! Who else

do you know broke a leg chasing *shikses?* Or came in his eye first time out? Or found a real live monkey right in the streets of New York, a girl with a passion for The Banana? Doctor, maybe other patients dream—with me, *everything happens.* I have a life *without* latent content. The dream thing *happens!* Doctor: *I couldn't get it up in the State of Israel!* How's *that* for symbolism, *bubi?* Let's see somebody beat that, for acting-out! Could not maintain an erection in The Promised Land! At least not when I needed it, not when I wanted it, not when there was something more desirable than my own hand to stick it into. But, as it turns out, you can't stick tapioca pudding into anything. Tapioca pudding I am offering this girl. Wet sponge cake! A thimbleful of something melted. And all the while that self-assured little lieutenant, so proudly flying those Israeli tits, prepared to be mounted by some tank commander!

RENÉ DESCARTES

❤

from MEDITATIONS

The theories of the seventeenth-century French mathematician and philosopher René Descartes (1596–1650) provided the basis for Rationalism. In keeping with his acceptance of truths that are not derived from experience, he was steadfast in his belief that some ideas are innate. He formulated the famous axiom *cogito, ergo sum* (I think, therefore I exist), which he took as irrefutable evidence of the existence of the mind. The principles of his philosophy were outlined in *Discourse on Method* and *Principles of Philosophy*.

*I*t may be said, perhaps, that, although the senses occasionally mislead us respecting minute objects, and such as are far removed from us as to be beyond the reach of close observation, there are yet many others their informations (presentations), of the truth of which it is manifestly impossible to doubt; as for example, that I am in this place, seated by the fire, clothed in a winter dressing-gown, that I hold in my hands this piece of paper, with other intimations of the same nature. But how could I deny that I possess these hands and this body, and withal escape being classed with persons in a state of insanity, whose brains are so disordered by dark bilious vapors to cause them pertinaciously to assert that they are monarch when they are in the greatest poverty. . . . I should certainly not be less insane than they, were I to regulate my procedure according to examples so extravagant.

Though this be true, I must nevertheless here consider that I am a man, and that, consequently, I am in the habit of sleeping, and representing to myself in dreams those same things, or even sometimes others less probable, which the insane think are presented to them in their waking moments. How often have I dreamt that I was in these familiar circumstances—that I was dressed, and occupied this place by the fire, when I was lying undressed in bed? At the present moment, however, I certainly look upon this paper with eyes wide awake; the head which I now move is not asleep; I extend this hand consciously and with express purpose, and I perceive it; the occurrences in sleep are not so distinct as all this. But I cannot forget that, at other times, I have been deceived in sleep by similar illusions; and, attentively considering those cases, I perceive so clearly that there exist no certain marks by which the state of waking can ever be distinguished from sleep, and that I feel greatly astonished; and in amazement I almost persuade myself that I am now dreaming.

Let us suppose, then, that we are dreaming, and that all those particulars—namely, the opening of the eyes, the motion of the head, the forth-putting of the hands—are merely illusions; and even that we really possess neither an entire body nor hands such as we see. Nevertheless, it must be admitted at least that the objects which appear to us in sleep are, as it were, painted representations which could not have been formed unless in the likeness of realities; and, therefore, that those general objects, at all events, namely, eyes, a head, hands, and an entire body—are not simply imaginary, but really existent. For, in truth, painters themselves, even when they study to represent sirens and satyrs by forms the most fantastic and extraordinary, cannot bestow upon them natures absolutely new, but can only make a certain medley of the members of different animals; or if they chance to imagine something so novel that nothing at all similar has ever been seen before, and such as is, therefore, purely fictitious and absolutely false, it is at least certain that the colors of which this is composed are real. . . .

Perception is another attribute of the soul; but perception too is impossible without the body; besides, I have frequently, during sleep, believed that I perceived objects which I afterwards observed I did not in reality perceive. Thinking is another attribute of the soul; and here I discover what properly belongs to myself. This alone is inseparable from me. I am—I exist: this is certain; but how often? As often as I think; for perhaps it would even happen, if I should wholly cease to think, that I should at the same time altogether cease to be. . . .

I am now awake, and perceive something real; but because my perception is not sufficiently clear, I will of express purpose go to sleep that my dreams may represent to me the object of my perception with more truth and clearness. And, therefore, I know that nothing of all that I can embrace in imagination belongs to the knowledge which I have got of myself, and that there is need to recall with the utmost care the mind from this mode of thinking, that it may be able to know its own nature with perfect distinctness.

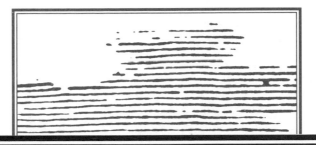

DESIRE AND LOVE

◘

"THE DREAM"

American poet Theodore Roethke (1908–1963) often touched upon familiar themes of life, love, and death expressed through his own intense personal experience. He is the recipient of several awards, including the Pulitzer Prize for *Collected Poems*, 1954. "The Dream" was originally published in *Words for the Wind*.

1

I met her as a blossom on a stem
Before she ever breathed, and in that dream
The mind remembers from a deeper sleep:
Eye learned from eye, cold lip from sensual lip.
My dream divided on a point of fire;
Light hardened on the water where we were;
A bird sang low; the moonlight sifted in;
The water rippled, and she rippled on.

2

She came toward me in the flowing air,
A shape of change, encircled by its fire.
I watched her there, between me and the moon;
The bushes and the stones danced on and on;
I touched her shadow when the light delayed;
I turned my face away, and yet she stayed.
A bird sang from the center of a tree;
She loved the wind because the wind loved me.

3

Love is not love until love's vulnerable.
She slowed to sigh, in that long interval.
A small bird flew in circles where we stood;
The deer came down, out of the dappled wood.
All who remember, doubt. Who calls that strange?
I tossed a stone, and listened to its plunge.
She knew the grammar of least motion, she
Lent me one virtue, and I live thereby.

4

She held her body steady in the wind;
Our shadows met, and slowly swung around;
She turned the field into a glittering sea;
I played in flame and water like a boy
And I swayed out beyond the white seafoam;
Like a wet log, I sang within a flame
In that last while, eternity's confine,
I came to love, I came into my own

D. M. THOMAS

✜

from THE WHITE HOTEL

In addition to *The White Hotel,* British novelist and poet D. M. Thomas's novels include *The Flute Player, Sphinx,* and *Pictures at an Exhibition;* he has also written several volumes of poetry and translated two volumes by the Russian poet Anna Akhmatova. *The White Hotel* traces the history of an imaginary patient of Freud's named Lisa Erdman. As her story unfolds through a variety of unconventional narrative forms we learn of the various events in Lisa's life and of her tragic destiny at Babi Yar. In this sequence, which is part dream and part violent sexual fantasy, the image and setting of the white hotel juxtapose the death instinct and the pleasure principle.

1

I dreamt of falling trees in a wild storm
I was between them as a desolate shore
came to meet me and I ran, scared stiff,
there was a trapdoor but I could not lift
it, I have started an affair
with your son, on a train somewhere
in a dark tunnel, his hand was underneath
my dress between my thighs I could not breathe
he took me to a white lakeside hotel
somewhere high up, the lake was emerald
I could not stop myself I was in flames
from the first spreading of my thighs, no shame
could make me push my dress down, thrust his hand

away, the two, then three, fingers he jammed
into me though the guard brushed the glass,
stopped for a moment, staring in, then passed
down the long train, his thrumming fingers filled
me with a great gape of wanting wanting till
he half supported me up the wide steps
into the vestibule where the concierge slept
so took the keys and ran up, up, my dress
above my hips not stopping to undress,
juices ran down my thighs, the sky was blue
but towards night a white wind blew
off the snowcapped mountain above the trees,
we stayed there, I don't know, a week at least
and never left the bed, I was split open
by your son, Professor, and now come back, a broken
woman, perhaps more broken, can
you do anything for me can you understand.

I think it was the second night, the wind
came rushing through the larches, hard as flint,
the summer-house pagoda roof came down,
billows were whipped up, and some people drowned,
we heard some waiters running and some guests
but your son kept his hand upon my breast
then plunged his mouth to it, the nipple swelled,
there were shouts and there were crashes in the hotel
we thought we were in a liner out to sea
a white liner, he kept sucking sucking me,
I wanted to cry, my nipples were so drawn
out by his lips, and tender, your son moved on
from one nipple to another, both were swollen,
I think some windowpanes were broken

☙

then he rammed in again you can't conceive
how pure the stars are, large as maple leaves
up in the mountains, they kept falling falling
into the lake, we heard some people calling,
we think the falling stars were Leonids,
and for a time one of his fingers slid
beside his prick in me there was such room,
set up a crosswise flutter, in the gloom
bodies were being brought to shore, we heard
a sound of weeping, his finger hurt
me jammed right up my arsehole my nail began
caressing where his prick so fat it didn't
belong to him any more was hidden
away in my cunt, came a lightning flash
a white zig-zag that went so fast
it was gone before the thunder cracked
over the hotel, then it was black
again with just a few lights on the lake,
I think the billiard room was flooded, we ached
he couldn't bring himself to let it gush
it was so beautiful, it makes me blush
now to be telling you, Professor, I
wasn't ashamed then, although I cried,
after about an hour he came inside,
we heard doors banging they were bringing in
the bodies from the lake, the wind
was very high still, we kept
our hands still on each other as we slept.

One evening they rescued a cat, its black fur
had been almost lost against the dark-green fir,
we stood naked by the window as a hand
searched among the foliage, it scratched,

it had been up there two days since the flood,
that was the night I felt a trickle of blood,
he was showing me some photographs, I said
Do you mind if the trees are turning red?
I don't mean that we literally never left
the bed, after the cat was taken down, we dressed
and went downstairs to eat, between the tables
there was a space to dance, I was unstable,
I had the dress I stood up in, no more,
I felt air on my flesh, the dress was short,
weakly I tried to push away his hand,
he said, I can't stop touching you, I can't,
please, you must let me, please,
couples were smiling at us indulgently,
he licked his glistening fingers as we sat,
I watched his red hand cut away the fat,
we ran down to the larches, I felt a cool
breeze blow on my skin and it was beautiful,
we couldn't hear the band in the hotel
though now and then some gypsy music swelled,
that night he almost burst my cunt apart
being tighter from my flow of blood, the stars
were huge over the lake, there was no room
for a moon, but the stars fell in our room,
and lit up the summer-house's fallen roof
pagoda-like, and sometimes the white cap
of the mountain was lit by a lightning flash.

2

One whole day, the servants made our bed.
Rising at dawn, we left the white hotel
to set sail in a yacht on the wide lake.
From dawn until the day began to fade

we sailed in our three-masted white-sailed craft.
Beneath our rug your son's right hand was jammed
up to the wrist inside me, laced in skin.
The sky was blue without a cloudy hint.
The white hotel merged into trees. The trees
merged into the horizon of green sea.
I said, Please fuck me, please. Am I too blunt?
I'm not ashamed. It was the murderous sun.
But there was nowhere in the ship to lie,
for everywhere there were people drinking wine
and gnawing chicken breasts. They gazed at us
two invalids who never left our rug.
I went into a kind of fever, so
besotted by your son's unresting stroke,
Professor, driving like a piston in
and out, hour after hour. It wasn't till
the sun drew in, that their gaze turned away,
not to the crimson sunset but the blaze
coming from our hotel, again in sight
between the tall pines. It outblazed the sky
—one wing was burning, and the people rushed
to the ship's prow to stare at it in horror.
So, pulling me upon him without warning,
your son impaled me, it was so sweet I screamed
but no one heard me for the other screams
as body after body fell or leapt
from upper storeys of the white hotel.
I jerked and jerked until his prick released
its cool soft flood. Charred bodies hung from trees,
he grew erect again, again I lunged,
oh I can't tell you how our rapture gushed,
the wing was gutted, you could see the beds,

we don't know how it started, someone said
it might have been the unaccustomed sun
driving through our opened curtains, kindling
our still-warm sheets, or (smoking was forbidden)
the maids, tired out, lighting up and drowsing,
or the strong burning-glass, the melting mountain.

I couldn't sleep that night, I was so sore,
I think something inside me had been torn,
your son was tender to me, deep in me
all night, but without moving. Women keened
out on the terrace where the bodies lay,
I don't know if you know the scarlet pain
of women, but I felt the shivers spread
hour after hour as the calm lake sent
dark ripples to the shores. By dawn, we had
not moved apart or slept. Asleep at last
I was the *Magdalen,* a figure-head,
plunging in deep seas. I was impaled
upon a swordfish and I drank the gale,
my wooden skin carved up by time, the wind
of icebergs where the northern lights begin.
The ice was soft at first, a whale who moaned
a lullaby to my corset, the thin bones,
I couldn't tell the wind from the lament
of whales, the hump of white bergs without end.
Then gradually it was the ice itself
cut into me, for we were an ice-breaker,
a breast was sheared away, I felt forsaken,
I gave birth to a wooden embryo
its gaping lips were sucking at the snow
as it was whirled away into the storm,

now turning inside-out the blizzard tore
my womb clean out, I saw it spin into
the whiteness have you seen a flying womb.

You can't imagine the relief it was
to wake and find the sun, already hot,
stroking the furniture with a serene
light, and your son watching me tenderly.
I was so happy both my breasts were there
I leapt out to the balcony. The air
was balmy with a scent of leaves and pines,
I leaned upon the rail, he came behind
and rammed up into me, he got so far
up into me, my still half-wintry heart
burst into sudden flower, I couldn't tell
which hole it was, I felt the white hotel
and even the mountains start to shake, black forks
sprang into sight where all was white before.

3
We made dear friends who died while we were there.
One was a woman, a corsetière,
who was as plump and jolly as her trade,
but the deep nights were ours alone. Stars rained
continuously and slowly like huge roses,
and once, a fragrant orange grove came floating
down past our window as we lay in awe,
our hearts were speechless as we saw them fall
extinguished with a hiss in the black lake,
a thousand lanterns hidden under drapes.
Don't imagine there were never times
of listening gently to the night's
tremendous silence, side by side, untouching,

or at least only his hand softly brushing
the mount he said reminded him of ferns
he hid and romped in as a boy. I learned
a lot about you from his whispers then,
you and his mother stood beside the bed.
Sunsets—the pink and drifting cloud-flowers, churning
off snowy peaks, the white hotel was turning,
my breasts were spinning into dusk, his tongue
churned every sunset in my barking cunt
and my throat drank his juice, it turned to milk,
or milk came into being for his lips,
for by the second night my breasts were bursting,
love in the afternoon had made us thirsty,
he drained a glass of wine and stretched across,
I opened up my dress, and my ache shot
a gush out even before his mouth had closed
upon my nipple, and I let the old
kind priest who dined with us take out the other,
the guests were gazing with a kind of wonder,
but smilingly, as if to say, you must,
for nothing in the white hotel but love
is offered at a price we can afford,
the chef stood beaming in the open door.
The milk was too much for two men, the chef
came through and held a glass under my breast,
draining it off he said that it was good,
we complimented him, the food was cooked
as tenderly as it had ever been,
more glasses came, the guests demanded cream,
and the hot thirsty band, the falling light
spread butter suddenly on the trees outside
the great french windows, butter on the lake,
the old kind priest kept sucking me, he craved

his mother who was dying in a slum,
my other breast fed other lips, your son's,
I felt his fingers underneath the table
stroking my thighs, my thighs were open, shaking.

We had to rush upstairs. His prick was up
me and my cunt began to flood
even before we reached the top, the priest
had left to lead the mourners through the trees
to the cold mountainside, we heard the chants
receding down the shore, he took my hand
and slid my fingers up beside him there,
our other friend the plump corsetière
slid hers in too, it was incredible,
so much in me, yet still I was not full,
they bore the bodies from the flood and fire
on carts, we heard them rumbling through the pines
and fade to silence, I pulled up her skirts
for she was so gripped by her belt, it hurt,
and let him finish it in her, it seemed
no different, for love ran without a seam
from lake to sky to mountain to our room,
we saw the line of mourners in the gloom
of the peak's shadow, standing by the trench,
a breeze brought in a memory of the scent
of orange groves and roses falling through
this universe of secrets, mothers swooned
crumpling into the muddy earth, a bell
tolled from the church behind the white hotel,
above it rather, half-way up the slope
to the observatory, words of hope
came floating from the priest, a lonely man
stood on the lake beside the nets, his hat

held to his breast, we heard a thunderclap,
the peak, held up a moment by their chants,
hung in mid-air, then fell, an avalanche
burying the mourners and the dead.
The echo died away, I shan't forget
the silence as it fell, a cataract
of darkness, for that night the white lake drank
the sunlight swiftly and there was no moon,
I think he penetrated to her womb
she screamed a joyful scream, and her teeth bit
my breast so hard it flowered beads of milk.

4

One evening when the lake was a red sheet,
we dressed, and climbed up to the mountain peak
behind the white hotel, up the rough path
zig-zagging between larches, pines, his hand
helped me in the climb, but also swayed
inside me, seeking me. When we had gained
the yew trees by the church we rested there;
grazing short grass, a tethered donkey stared,
an old nun with a basket of soiled clothes
came, as he glided in, and said, The cold
spring here will take away all sin,
don't stop. It was the spring that fed the lake
the sun drew up to fall again as rain.
She washed the clothes. We scrambled up the slope
into the region of eternal cold
above the trees. The sun dropped, just in time,
we entered the observatory, blind.
I don't know if you know how much your son
admires the stars, the stars are in his blood,
but when we gazed up through the glass there were

no stars at all, the stars had gone to earth;
I didn't know till then the stars, in flakes
of snow, come down to fuck the earth, the lake.
It was too dark to reach the white hotel
that night, and so we fucked again, and slept.
I felt the ghostly images of him
cascading, and I heard the mountains sing,
for mountains when they meet sing songs like whales.

The whole night sky came down that night, in flakes,
we lay in such high silence that we heard
the joyful sighs of when the universe
began to come, so many years ago,
at dawn when we crunched stars to drink the snow
everything was white, the lake as well,
the white hotel was lost, until he turned
the glass down towards the lake and saw the words
I'd written on our window with my breath.
He moved the glass and we saw edelweiss
rippling in a distant mountain's ice,
he pointed where some parachutists fell
between two peaks, we saw the sunlight flash
in the now heavenly blue, a corset clasp,
it was our friend, there was the lilac bruise
his thumb had printed in her thigh, the sight
excited him I think, my light
head felt him burst up through, the cable car
hung on a strand, swung in the wind, my heart
was fluttering madly and I screamed, the guests
fell through the sky, his tongue drummed at my breast,
I've never known my nipples grow so quickly,
the women fell more slowly, almost drifting,
because their petticoats and skirts were galing,

the men fell through them, my heart was breaking,
the women seemed to rise not fall, a dance
in which the men were lifting in light hands
light ballerinas high above their heads,
the men were first to come to ground, and then
the women fell into the lake or trees,
silently followed by a few bright skis.

On our way down we rested by the spring.
Strangely from so high we saw the fish
clearly in the lucid lake, a million
gliding darting fins of gold or silver
reminding me of the sperm seeking my womb.
Some of the fish were nuzzling guests for food.
Am I too sexual? I sometimes think
I am obsessed by it, it's not as if
God fills the waters with mad spawning shapes
or loads the vine with grapes, the palm with dates,
or makes the hull dilate to take the peach
or the plum tremble at the ox's reek
or the sun cover the pale moon. Your son
crashed through my modesty, a stag in rut.
The staff were wonderful. I've never known
such service as they gave, the telephones
were never still, nor the reception bell,
honeymoon couples, begging for a bed,
had to be turned away, as guests moved out
a dozen more moved in, they found
a corner for a couple we heard weeping
at being turned away, we heard her screaming
somewhere the next night, the birth beginning,
waiters and maids were running with warm linen.
The burnt-out wing was built again in days,

the staff all helped, one morning when my face
lay buried in the pillow, and my rump
taking his thrusts was coming in a flood
we heard a scraping, at the window was
the jolly chef, his face was beaming, hot,
he gave the wood a fresh white coat, and winked,
I didn't mind which one of them was in,
the steaks he cooked were rare and beautiful,
the juice was natural, and it was good
to feel a part of me was someone else,
no one was selfish in the white hotel
where waters of the lake could lap the screes
of mountains that the wild swans soared between,
their down so snowy-white the peaks seemed grey,
or glided down between them to the lake.

SIGMUND FREUD

❈

from "ON DREAMS"

The originator of modern psychoanalysis, Sigmund Freud (1856–1939) was one of the first psychologists to use dream interpretation as an analytic tool. He recognized in the symbolic content of dreams a means to tap into his patients' repressed emotions. His *The Interpretation of Dreams,* published in 1900, was revolutionary as a study of the subconscious.

*N*o one who accepts the view that the censorship is the chief reason for dream-distortion will be surprised to learn from the results of dream-interpretation that most of the dreams of adults are traced back by analysis to *erotic wishes.* This assertion is not aimed at dreams with an *undisguised* sexual content, which are no doubt familiar to all dreamers from their own experience and are as a rule the only ones to be described as 'sexual dreams'. Even dreams of this latter kind offer enough surprises in their choice of the people whom they make into sexual objects, in their disregard of all the limitations which the dreamer imposes in his waking life upon his sexual desires, and by their many strange details, hinting at what are commonly known as 'perversions'. A great many other dreams, however, which show no sign of being erotic in their manifest content, are revealed by the work of interpretation in analysis as sexual wish-fulfilments; and, on the other hand, analysis proves that a great many of the thoughts left over from the activity of waking life as 'residues of the previous day' only find their way to representation in dreams through the assistance of repressed erotic wishes.

There is no theoretical necessity why this should be so; but to explain the fact it may be pointed out that no other group of instincts has been submitted to such far-reaching suppression by the demands of cultural education, while at the same time the sexual instincts are also the ones which, in most people, find it easiest to escape from the control of the highest mental agencies. Since we have become acquainted with infantile sexuality, which is often so unobtrusive in its manifestations and is always overlooked and misunderstood, we are justified in saying that almost every civilized man retains the infantile forms of sexual life in some respect or other. We can thus understand how it is that repressed infantile sexual wishes provide the most frequent and strongest motive-forces for the construction of dreams.

There is only one method by which a dream which expresses erotic wishes can succeed in appearing innocently non-sexual in its manifest content. The material of the sexual ideas must not be represented as such, but must be replaced in the content of the dream by hints, allusions and similar forms of indirect representation. But, unlike other forms of indirect representation, that which is employed in dreams must not be immediately intelligible. The modes of representation which fulfil these conditions are usually described as 'symbols' of the things which they represent. Particular interest has been directed to them since it has been noticed that dreamers speaking the same language make use of the same symbols, and that in some cases, indeed, the use of the same symbols extends beyond the use of the same language. Since dreamers themselves are unaware of

⚬

the meaning of the symbols they use, it is difficult at first sight to discover the source of the connection between the symbols and what they replace and represent. The fact itself, however, is beyond doubt, and it is important for the technique of dream-interpretation. For, with the help of a knowledge of dream-symbolism, it is possible to understand the meaning of separate elements of the content of a dream or separate pieces of a dream or in some cases even whole dreams, without having to ask the dreamer for his associations. Here we are approaching the popular ideal of translating dreams and on the other hand are returning to the technique of interpretation used by the ancients, to whom dream-interpretation was identical with interpretation by means of symbols.

Although the study of dream-symbols is far from being complete, we are in a position to lay down with certainty a number of general statements and a quantity of special information on the subject. There are some symbols which bear a single meaning almost universally: thus the Emperor and Empress (or the King and Queen) stand for the parents, rooms represent women and their entrances and exits the openings of the body. The majority of dream-symbols serve to represent persons, parts of the body and activities invested with erotic interest; in particular, the genitals are represented by a number of often very surprising symbols, and the greatest variety of objects are employed to denote them symbolically. Sharp weapons, long and stiff objects, such as tree-trunks and sticks, stand for the male genital; while cupboards, boxes, carriages or ovens may represent the uterus. In such cases as these the *tertium comparationis,* the common element in these substitutions, is immediately intelligible; but there are other symbols in which it is not so easy to grasp the connection. Symbols such as a staircase or going upstairs to represent sexual intercourse, a tie or cravat for the male organ, or wood for the female one, provoke our unbelief until we can arrive at an understanding of the symbolic relation underlying them by some other means. Moreover a whole number of dream-symbols are bisexual and can relate to the male or female genitals according to the context.

Some symbols are universally disseminated and can be met with in all dreamers belonging to a single linguistic or cultural group; there are others which occur only within the most restricted and individual limits, symbols constructed by an individual out of his own ideational material. Of the former class we can distinguish some whose claim to represent sexual ideas is immediately justified by linguistic usage (such, for instance, as those derived from agriculture, e.g. 'fertilization' or 'seed') and others whose relation to sexual ideas appears to reach back into the very earliest ages and to the most obscure depths of our conceptual functioning. The power of constructing symbols has not been exhausted in our own days in the case of either of the two sorts of symbols which I have distinguished at the beginning of this paragraph. Newly discovered objects (such as airships) are, as we may observe, at once adopted as universally available sexual symbols.

It would, incidentally, be a mistake to expect that if we had a still profounder knowledge of dream-symbolism (of the 'language of dreams') we could do without asking the dreamer for his associations to the dream and go back entirely to the technique of dream-interpretation of antiquity. Quite apart from individual symbols and oscillations in the use of universal ones, one can never tell whether any particular element in the content of a dream is to be interpreted symbolically or in its proper sense, and one can be certain that the *whole* content of a dream is not to be interpreted symbolically. A knowledge of dream-symbolism will never do more than enable us to translate certain constituents of the dream-content, and will not relieve us of the necessity for applying the technical rules which I gave earlier. It will, however, afford the most valuable assistance to interpretation precisely at points at which the dreamer's associations are insufficient or fail altogether.

Dream-symbolism is also indispensable to an understanding of what are known as 'typical' dreams, which are common to everyone, and of 'recurrent' dreams in individuals.

We must not suppose that dream-symbolism is a creation of the dream-work; it is in all probability a characteristic of the unconscious thinking which provides the dream-work with the material for condensation, displacement and dramatization.

❦

"THE NIGHT DREAM"

Involved in many of the political movements of his era, Archibald MacLeish (1892–1982) wrote numerous social and political essays; and he often incorporated political messages into his verse. During the second world war, the Pulitzer Prize–winning poet held several positions within the federal government. He is probably best remembered, however, for his lyric poems, which often touched on more classical themes. "The Night Dream" was originally published in *Poems, 1924–1933*.

to R. L.

*N*either her voice, her name,
Eyes, quietness neither,
That moved through the light, that came
Cold stalk in her teeth
Bitten of some blue flower
Knew I before nor saw.
This was a dream. Ah,
This was a dream. There was sun
Laid on the cloths of a table.
We drank together. Her mouth
Was a lion's mouth out of jade
Cold with a fable of water.
Faces I could not see
Watched me with gentleness. Grace
Folded my body with wings.

I cannot love you she said.
My head she laid on her breast.
As stillness with ringing of bees
I was filled with a singing of praise.
Knowledge filled me and peace.
We were silent and not ashamed.
Ah we were glad that day.
They asked me but it was one
Dead they meant and not I
She was beside me she said.
We rode in a desert place.
We were always happy. Her sleeves
Jangled with jingling of gold.
They told me the wind from the south
Was the cold wind to be feared.
We were galloping under the leaves—

This was a dream, Ah
This was a dream.
                And her mouth
Was not your mouth nor her eyes,
But the rivers were four and I knew
As a secret between us, the way
Hands touch, it was you.

EDNA O'BRIEN

⚮

"NUMBER 10"

An Irish novelist and short-story writer noted for exploring passionate subjects through carefully crafted prose, Edna O'Brien's novels include *Night* and *House of Splendid Isolation*. Her story collections include *The Love Object, Lantern Slides,* and *A Fanatic Heart*. "Number 10" is taken from *A Fanatic Heart*.

*E*verything began to be better for Mrs. Reinhardt from the moment she started to sleepwalk. Every night her journey yielded a fresh surprise. First it was that she saw sheep—not sheep as one sees them in life, a bit sooty and bleating away, but sheep as one sees them in a dream. She saw myriads of white fleece on a hilltop, surrounded by little lambs frisking and suckling to their heart's content.

Then she saw pictures such as she had not seen in life. Her husband owned an art gallery and Mrs. Reinhardt had the opportunity to see many pictures, yet the ones she saw at night were much more satisfying. For one thing, she was inside them. She was not an outsider looking in, making idiotic remarks, she was part of the picture: an arm or a lily or the gray mane of a horse. She did not have to compete, did not have to say anything. All her movements were preordained. She was simply aware of her own breath, a soft steady, sustaining breath.

In the mornings her husband would say she looked a bit frayed or a bit intense, and she would say, "Nonsense," because in twenty years of marriage she had never felt better. Her sleeping life suited her, and of course, she never knew what to expect. Her daily life had a pattern to it. Weekday mornings she spent at home, helping or supervising Fatima, the Spanish maid. She gave two afternoons a week to teaching autistic children, two afternoons were devoted to an exercise class, and on Fridays she shopped in Harrods and got all the groceries for the weekend. Mr. Reinhardt had bought a farm two years before, and weekends they spent in the country, in their newly renovated cottage. In the country she did not sleepwalk, and Mrs. Reinhardt wondered if it might be that she was inhibited by the barbed-wire fence that skirted their garden. But there are gates, she thought, and I should open them. She was a little vexed with herself for not being more venturesome.

Then one May night, back in her house in London, she had an incredible dream. She walked over a field with her son—in real life he was at university—and all of a sudden, and in unison, the two of them knelt down and began scraping the earth up with their bare hands. It was a rich red earth and easy to crumble. They were so eager because they knew that treasure was about to be theirs. Sure enough, they found bits of gold, tiny specks of it which they put in a handkerchief, and then, to crown her happiness, Mrs. Reinhardt found the loveliest little gold key and held it up to the light while her son laughed and in a baby voice said, "Mama."

Soon after this dream Mrs. Reinhardt embarked on a bit of spring cleaning. Curtains and carpets for the dry cleaner's, drawers depleted of all the old useless odds and ends that had been piling up. Her husband's clothing, too, she must put in order. A little rift had sprung up between them and was widening day by day. He was moody. He got home later than usual, and though he did not say so, she knew that he had

stopped at the corner and had a few drinks. Once that spring
he had pulled her down beside him on the living-room sofa
and stroked her thighs and started to undress her within
hearing distance of Fatima, who was in the kitchen chopping
and singing. Always chopping and singing or humming. For
the most part, though, Mr. Reinhardt went straight to the
liquor cabinet and gave them both a gin, pouring himself a
bigger one because, as he said, all her bloody fasting made
Mrs. Reinhardt lightheaded.

She was sorting Mr. Reinhardt's shirts—T-shirts, summer sweaters, thick crew-neck sweaters—and putting them
each in a neat pile, when out of his seersucker jacket there
tumbled a little gold key that caused her to let out a cry. The
first thing she felt was a jet of fear. Then she bent down and
picked it up. It was exactly like the one in her sleepwalk.
She held it in her hand, promising herself never to let it go.
What fools we are to pursue in daylight what we should leave
for nighttime.

Her next sleepwalking brought Mrs. Reinhardt out of her
house into a waiting taxi and, some distance away, to a mews
house. Outside the mews house was a black-and-white tub
filled with pretty flowers. She simply put her hand under a
bit of foliage and there was the latchkey. Inside was a little
nest. The wallpaper in the hall was the very one she had
always wanted for their house, a pale gold with the tiniest
white flowers—mere suggestions of flowers, like those of the
wild strawberry. The kitchen was immaculate. On the landing upstairs was a little fretwork bench. The cushions in the
sitting room were stiff and stately, and so was the upholstery,
but the bedroom—ah, the bedroom.

It was everything she had ever wanted their own to be.
In fact, the bedroom was the very room she had envisaged
over and over again and had described to her husband down

to the last detail. Here it was—a brass bed with a little lace canopy above it, the entire opposite wall a dark metallic mirror in which dark shadows seemed to swim around, a light-blue velvet chaise longue, a hanging plant with shining leaves, and a floor lamp with an amber shade that gave off the softest of light.

She sat on the edge of the bed, marveling, and saw the other things that she had always wanted. She saw, for instance, the photo of a little girl in First Communion attire; she saw the paperweight that when shaken yielded a miniature snowstorm; she saw the mother-of-pearl tray with the two champagne glasses—and all of a sudden she began to cry, because her happiness was so immense. Perhaps, she thought, he will come to me here, he will visit, and it will be like the old days and he won't be irritable and he won't be tapping with his fingers or fiddling with the lever of his fountain pen. He will smother me with hugs and kisses and we will tumble about on the big bed.

She sat there in the bedroom and she touched nothing, not even the two white irises in the tall glass vase. The little key was in her hand and she knew it was for the wardrobe and that she had only to open it to find there a nightdress with a pleated top, a voile dance dress, a silver-fox cape, and a pair of sling-back shoes. But she did not open it. She wanted to leave something a secret. She crept away and was home in her own bed without her husband being aware of her absence. He had complained on other occasions about her cold feet as she got back into bed, and asked in Christ's name what was she doing—making tea or what? That morning her happiness was so great that she leaned over, unknotted his pyjamas, and made love to him very sweetly, very slowly, and to his apparent delight. Yet when he wakened he was angry, as if a wrong had been done him.

Naturally, Mrs. Reinhardt now went to the mews house night after night, and her heart would light up as she saw the pillar of the house with its number, 10, lettered in gold edged with black. Sometimes she slipped into the brass bed, knowing it was only a question of time before Mr. Reinhardt followed her there.

One night as she lay in the bed, a little breathless, he came in very softly, closed the door, removed his dressing gown, and took possession of her with such a force that afterward she suspected she had a broken rib. They used words that they had not used for years. She was young and wild. A lovely fever took hold of her. She was saucy while he kept imploring her to please marry him, to please give up her independence, to please be his—adding that even if she said no, he was going to whisk her off. Then to prove his point he took possession of her again. She almost died, so deep and so thorough was her pleasure, and each time, as she came back to her senses, she saw some little object or trinket that was intended to add to her pleasure—once it was a mobile in which silver horses chased one another around, once it was a sound as of a running stream. He gave her some champagne and they drank in utter silence.

But when she wakened from this idyll she was in fact in her own bed and so was he. She felt mortified. Had she cried out in her sleep? Had she moaned? There was no rib broken. She reached for the hand mirror and saw no sign of wantonness on her face, no tossed hair, and the buttons of her nightdress were neatly done up to the throat.

He was a solid mass of sleep. He opened his eyes. She said something to him, something anxious, but he did not reply. She got out of bed and went down to the sitting room to think. Where would it all lead to? Should she tell him? She thought not. All morning she tried the key in different locks, but it was too small. In fact, once she nearly lost it because it slipped into a lock and she had to tease it out with the prong of a fork. Of course, she did not let Fatima, the maid, see what she was doing.

It was Friday, their day to go to the country, and she was feeling reluctant about it. She knew that when they arrived they would rush around their garden and look at their plants to see if they'd thrived, and look at the rose leaves to make sure there was no green fly. Then, staring out across the fields to where the cows were, they would tell each other how lucky they were to have such a nice place, and how clever. The magnolia flowers would be fully out, and she would stand and stare at the tree as if by staring at it she could imbue her body with something of its whiteness.

The magnolias were out when they arrived—like little white china eggcups, each bloom lifted to the heavens. Two of the elms definitely had the blight, Mr. Reinhardt said, as the leaves were withering away. The elms would have to be chopped, and Mr. Reinhardt estimated that there would be enough firewood for two winters. He would speak to the farm manager, who lived down the road, about this. They carried in the shopping, raised the blinds, and switched on the central heating. The little kitchen was just as they had left it, except that the primroses in the jar had faded and were like bits of yellow skin. She unpacked the food they had brought, put some things in the fridge, and began to peel the carrots and potatoes for the evening meal. Mr. Reinhardt hammered four picture hangers into the wall for the new prints that he had brought down. From time to time he would call her to ask what order he should put them in, and she would go in, her hands covered with flour, and rather absently suggest a grouping.

She had the little key with her in her purse and would open the purse from time to time to make sure that it was there. Then she would blush.

At dusk she went out to get a branch of apple wood for the fire, in order to engender a lovely smell. A bird chirped from a tree. It was more sound than song. She could not tell what bird it was. The magnolia tree was a mass of white in the surrounding darkness. The dew was falling and she bent for a moment to touch the wet grass. She wished it were Sunday, so that they could be going home. In London the evenings seemed to pass more quickly and they each had more chores to do. She felt in some way she was deceiving him.

They drank some red wine as they sat by the fire. Mr. Reinhardt was fidgety but at the very same time accused her of being fidgety. He was being adamant about the Common Market. Why did he expound on the logistics of it when she was not even contradicting him? He got carried away, made gestures, said he loved England, loved it passionately, that England was going to the dogs. When she got up to push in a log that had fallen from the grate, he asked her for God's sake to pay attention.

She sat down at once, and hoped that there was not going to be one of those terrible, unexpected, meaningless rows. But blessedly they were distracted. She heard him say "Crikey!" and then she looked up and saw what he had just seen. There was a herd of cattle staring in at them. She jumped up. Mr. Reinhardt rushed to the phone to call the farm manager, since he himself knew nothing about country life, certainly not how to drive away cattle.

She grabbed a walking stick and went outside to prevent the cows from falling in the swimming pool. It was cold outdoors and the wind rustled in all the trees. The cows looked at her, suspicious. Their ears pricked. She made tentative movements with the stick, and at that moment four of them leaped over the barbed wire and back into the adjoining field. The remaining cow began to race around. From the field the four cows began to bawl. The fifth cow was butting against the paling. Mrs. Reinhardt thought, I know what you are feeling—you are feeling lost and muddled, and you have gone astray.

Her husband came out in a frenzy, because when he had rung the farm manager no one was there. "Bloody never there!" he said. His loud voice so frightened the poor cow that she made a leap for it and got stuck in the barbed wire. Mrs. Reinhardt could see the barb in her huge udder and thought, What a place for it to have landed. They must rescue her. Very cautiously they both approached the animal; the intention was that Mr. Reinhardt would hold the cow while Mrs. Reinhardt freed the flesh. She tried to be gentle. The cow's smell was milky and soft compared with her roar, which was beseeching. Mr. Reinhardt caught hold of the hindquarters and told his wife to hurry up. The cow was bucking. As Mrs. Reinhardt lifted the bleeding flesh away, the cow took a high jump and was over the fence and down the field, where she hurried to the river to drink.

The others followed her, and suddenly the whole meadow was the scene of bawling and mad commotion. Mr. Reinhardt rubbed his hands and let out a sigh of relief. He suggested that they open a bottle of champagne. Mrs. Reinhardt was delighted. Of late he had become very thrifty and did not permit her any extravagances. In fact, he had been saying that they would soon have to give up wine because of the state of the country. As they went indoors he put an arm around her. And back in the room she sat and felt like a mistress as she drank the champagne, smiled at him, and felt the stuff coursing through her body. The champagne put them in a nice mood and they linked as they went up the narrow stairs to bed. Nevertheless, Mrs. Reinhardt did not feel like any intimacy; she wanted it reserved for the hidden room.

They returned to London on Sunday evening, and that night Mrs. Reinhardt did not sleep. Consequently she walked nowhere in her dreams. In the morning she felt fidgety. She looked in the mirror. She was getting old. After breakfast, as Mr. Reinhardt was hurrying out of the house, she held up the little key.

"What is it?" she said.

"How would I know," he said. He looked livid.

She called and made an appointment at the hairdresser's. She addressed herself. She must not get old. Later when her hair was set she would surprise him—she would drop in at his gallery and ask him to take her to a nice pub. On the way she would buy a new scarf and knot it at the neck and she would be youthful.

When she got to the gallery, Mr. Reinhardt was not there. Hans, his assistant, was busy with a client from the Middle East. She said she would wait. The new secretary went off to make some tea. Mrs. Reinhardt sat at her husband's desk, brooding, and then idly she began to flick through his desk diary, just to pass the time. Lunch with this one and that one. A reminder to buy her a present for their anniversary— which he had done. He had bought her a beautiful ring with a sphinx on it.

Then she saw it—the address that she went to night after night. Number 10. The digits danced before her eyes as they had danced when she drove up in the taxi the very first time. All her movements became hurried and mechanical. She gulped her tea, she gave a distracted handshake to the Arab gentleman, she ate the ginger biscuit and gnashed her teeth, so violently did she chew. She paced the floor, she went back

❧

to the diary. The same address—three, four, or five times a week. She flicked back to see how long it had been going on. It was no use. She simply had to go there.

At the mews, she found the key in the flower tub. In the kitchen were eggshells and a pan in which an omelette had been cooked. There were two brown eggshells and one white. She dipped her finger in the fat; it was still warm. Her heart went ahead of her up the stairs. It was like a pellet in her body. She had her hand on the bedroom doorknob, when all of a sudden she stopped in her tracks and became motionless. She crept away from the door and went back to the landing seat.

She would not intrude, no. It was perfectly clear why Mr. Reinhardt went there. He went by day to keep his tryst with her, be unfaithful with her, just as she went by night. One day or one night, if they were very lucky, they might meet and share their secret, but until then Mrs. Reinhardt was content to leave everything just as it was. She tiptoed down the stairs and was pleased that she had not acted rashly, that she had not broken the spell.

JAMES MERRILL

✢

"THE MAD SCENE"

James Merrill (1926–1995), an American poet, novelist, and playwright, is noted for his polished, sophisticated verse. He often
brought a large degree of wit to the metaphysical subjects of his
poems. In "The Mad Scene," he uses a dream to convey the destructive complexities of love. This was originally published in *Nights and
Days*, 1960.

Again last night I dreamed the dream called Laundry.
In it, the sheets and towels of a life we were going to share,
The milk-stiff bibs, the shroud, each rag to be ever
Trampled or soiled, bled on or groped for blindly,
Came swooning out of an enormous willow hamper
Onto moon-marbly boards. We had just met. I watched
From outer darkness. I had dressed myself in clothes
Of a new fiber that never stains or wrinkles, never
Wears thin. The opera house sparkled with tiers
And tiers of eyes, like mine enlarged by belladonna,
Trained inward. There I saw the cloud-clot, gust by gust,
Form, and the lightning bite, and the roan mare unloosen.
Fingers were running in panic over the flute's nine gates.
Why did I flinch? I loved you. And in the downpour laughed
To have us wrung white, gnarled together, one
Topmost mordent of wisteria,
as the lean tree burst into grief.

HARUKI MURAKAMI

✖

from DANCE DANCE DANCE

Born in Kyoto, Haruki Murakami is an imaginative writer who often incorporates aspects of contemporary American pop culture in his fiction. He is the author of *A Wild Sheep Chase* and *Hard-Boiled Wonderland and the End of the World.*

Yumiyoshi came back at six-thirty. Still in uniform, although her blouse was different. She'd brought a bag with a change of clothes and toiletries and cosmetics.

"I don't know," I said. "They're going to find out some time."

"Don't worry, I'm not careless," she said, then smiled and draped her blazer over the back of a chair.

Then we sat on the sofa and held each other tight.

"I've thought about you all day long," she said. "You know, wouldn't it be wonderful if I could work during the daytime, then sneak into your room at night? We'd spend the night together, then in the morning I'd go straight to work?"

"A home convenient to your workplace," I joked. "Unfortunately I couldn't keep footing the tab to this room. And sooner or later, they'll find out about us."

"Nothing goes smoothly in this world."

"You can say that again."

"But it'd be okay for a few more nights, wouldn't it?"

"I imagine that's what's going to happen."

"Good. I'll be happy with those few days. Let's both stay in this hotel."

Then she undressed, neatly folding each article of clothing. She removed her watch and her glasses, and placed them on the table. Then we enjoyed an hour of lovemaking, until we were both exhausted. No better kind of exhaustion.

"Mmm," was Yumiyoshi's appraisal. Then she snuggled up in my arms for a nap. After a while, I got up, showered, then drank a beer. I sat, admiring Yumiyoshi's sleeping face. She slept so nice.

A little before eight, she awoke, hungry. We ordered a sandwich and pasta au gratin from room service. Meanwhile, she stored her things in the closet, and when the bellhop knocked, she hid in the bathroom.

We ate happily.

"I've been thinking about it all afternoon," I began, picking up from our earlier conversation. "There's nothing for me in Tokyo anymore. I could move up here and look for work."

"You'd live here?"

"That's right, I'd live here," I said.

"I'll rent an apartment and start a new life here. You can come over whenever you want to. You can spend the night if you feel like it. We can try it out like that for a while. But I've got the feeling it's going to work out. It'll bring me back to reality. It'll give you space to relax. And it'll keep us together."

Yumiyoshi smiled and gave me a big kiss. "*Fan*tastic!"

"What comes later, I don't know. But I've got a good feeling about it. Like I said."

"Nobody knows what's going to happen in the future. I'm not worried about that. Right now, it's just fantastic! Oooh, the best kind of fantastic!"

I called room service for a bucket of ice, making Yumiyoshi hide in the bathroom again. And while she was in there, I took out the bottle of vodka and tomato juice I'd bought in town that afternoon and made us two Bloody Marys. No lemon slices or Lea & Perrins, but bloody good enough. We toasted. To us. I switched on the bedside Muzak and punched the Pops channel. Soon we were treated to the lush strains of Mantovani playing "Strangers in the Night." You didn't hear me making snide comments.

"You think of everything," said Yumiyoshi. "I was just dreaming of a Bloody Mary right about now. How did you know?"

"If you listen carefully, you can hear these things. If you look carefully, you'll see what you're after."

"Words of wisdom?"

"No, just words. A way of life in words."

"You ought to specialize in inspirational writing."

We had three Bloody Marys each. Then we took our clothes off and gently made love again.

At one point, in the middle of our lovemaking, I thought I could hear that old Dolphin Hotel elevator *cr-cr-crr-creaking* up the shaft. Yes, this place was the knot, the node. Here's where it all tied together and I was a part of it all. Here was reality, I didn't have to go further. I was already there. All I had to do was to recover the knot to be connected. It's what I'd been seeking for years. What the Sheep Man held together.

At midnight, we fell asleep.

Yumiyoshi was shaking me. "Wake up," she said urgently. Outside it was dark. My head was half full with the warm sludge of unconsciousness. The bedside light was on. The clock read a little after three.

❧

She was dressed in her hotel uniform, clutching my shoulder, shaking me, looking very serious. My first thought was that her boss had found out about us.

"Wake up. Please, wake up," she said.

"I'm awake," I said. "What is it?"

"Hurry up and get dressed."

I quickly slipped on a T-shirt and jeans and windbreaker, then stepped into my sneakers. It didn't take a minute. Then Yumiyoshi led me by hand to the door, and parted it open a scant two or three centimeters.

"Look," she said. I peeked through the opening. The hallway was pitch black. I couldn't see a thing. The darkness was thick, gelatinous, chill. It seemed so deep that if you stuck out a hand, you'd get sucked in. And then there was that familiar smell of mold, like old paper. A smell that had been brewed in the pit of time.

"It's that darkness again," she said.

I put my arm around her waist and drew her close. "It's nothing to be afraid of," I said. "Don't be scared. Nothing bad is going to happen. This is my world. The first time you ever talked to me was because of this darkness. That's how we got to know each other. Really, it's all right."

And yet I wasn't so sure. In fact, I was terrified out of my skin. Thoroughly unhinged, despite my own calm talk. The fear was palpable, fundamental; it was universal, historical, genetic. For darkness terrifies. It swallows you, warps you, nullifies you. Who alive can possibly profess confidence in darkness? In the dark, you can't *see*. Things can twist, turn, vanish. The essence of darkness—nothingness—covers all.

"It's okay," I was now trying to convince myself. "Nothing to be afraid of."

"So what do we do?" asked Yumiyoshi.

I went and quickly got the penlight and Bic lighter I'd brought just in case this very thing happened.

"We have to go through it together," I said. "I returned to this hotel to see two people. You were one. The other is a guy standing somewhere out there in the dark. He's waiting for me."

"The person who was in that room?"

"Yes."

"I'm scared. I'm *really* scared," said Yumiyoshi, trembling. Who could blame her?

I kissed her on her brow. "Don't be afraid. I'm with you. Give me your hand. If we don't let go, we'll be safe. No matter what happens, we mustn't let go. You understand? We have to stay together." Then we stepped into the corridor.

"Which way do we go?" she asked nervously.

"To the right," I said. "Always to the right."

We shined the light at our feet and walked, slowly, deliberately. As before, the corridor was no longer in the new Dolphin Hotel. The red carpet was worn, the floor sagging, the plaster walls stained with liver spots. It was *like* the old Dolphin Hotel, though it was *not* the old Dolphin Hotel. A little ways on, as before, the corridor turned right. We turned, but now something was different. There was no light ahead, no door leaking candlelight. I switched off my penlight to be certain. No light at all, none.

Yumiyoshi held my hand tightly.

"Where's that door?" I said, my voice sounding dry and dead, hardly my voice at all. "Before when I—"

"Me too. I saw a door somewhere."

We stood there at the turn in the corridor. What happened to the Sheep Man? Was he asleep? Wouldn't he have left the light on? As a beacon? Wasn't that the whole reason he was here? What the hell's going on?

❧

"Let's go back," Yumiyoshi said. "I don't like the darkness. We can try again another time. I don't want to press our luck."

She had a point. I didn't like the darkness either, and I had the foreboding feeling that something had gone awry. Yet I refused to give up.

"Let's keep going," I said. "The guy might need us. That's why we're still tied to this world." I switched the penlight back on. A narrow beam of yellow light pierced the darkness. "Hold on to my hand now. I need to know we're together. But there's nothing to be afraid of. We're staying, we're not going away. We'll get back safe and sound."

Step by step, even more slowly and deliberately, we went forward. The faint scent of Yumiyoshi's hair drifted through the darkness, sweetly pricking my senses. Her hand was small and warm and solid.

And then we saw it. The door to the Sheep Man's room had been left slightly ajar, and through the opening we could feel the old chill, smell the dank odor. I knocked. As before, the knock sounded unnaturally loud. Three times I knocked. Then we waited. Twenty seconds, thirty seconds. No response. Where is he? What's going on? Don't tell me he died! True, the guy was not looking well the last time we met. He couldn't live forever. He too had to grow old and die. But if he died, who would keep me connected to this world?

I pushed the door open and pulled Yumiyoshi with me into the room. I shined my penlight around. The room had not changed. Old books and papers piled everywhere, a tiny table, and on it the plate used as a candle stand, with a five-centimeter stub of wax on it. I used my Bic to light it.

The Sheep Man was not here.

Had he stepped out for a second?

"Who was this guy?" asked Yumiyoshi.

❁

"The Sheep Man," I said. "He takes care of this world here. He sees that things are tied together, makes sure connections are made. He said he was kind of like a switchboard. He's ages old, and he wears a sheepskin. This is where he's been living. In hiding."

"In hiding from what?"

"From war, civilization, the law, the system, . . . things that aren't Sheep Man–like."

"But he's not here. He's gone."

I nodded. And as I did a huge shadow bowed across the wall. "Yes, he's gone. Even though he's supposed to be here."

We were at the edge of the world. That is, what the ancients considered the edge of the world, where everything spilled over into nothingness. We were there, the two of us, alone. And all around us, a cold, vast void. We held each other's hand more tightly.

"Maybe he's dead," I said.

"How can you say a thing like that in the dark? Think more positively," said Yumiyoshi. "He could be off shopping, right? He probably ran out of candles."

"Or else he's gone to collect his tax refund." Even in the candlelit gloom I could see Yumiyoshi smile. We hugged each other. "You know," I said, "on our days off, let's drive to lots of places."

"Sure," she said.

"I'll ship my Subaru up. It's an old car, but it's a good car. It runs just fine. I like it better than a Maserati. I really do."

"Of course," she said. "Let's go everywhere and see lots of things together."

We embraced a little longer. Then Yumiyoshi stooped to pick up a pamphlet from the pile of papers that was lying at her feet. *Studies in the Varietal Breeding of Yorkshire Sheep.* It was browned with age, covered with dust.

⚓

"Everything in this room has to do with sheep," I explained. "In the old Dolphin Hotel, a whole floor was devoted to sheep research. There was this Sheep Professor, who was the father of the hotel manager. And I guess the Sheep Man inherited all this stuff. It's not good for anything anymore. Nobody's ever going to read this stuff. Still, the Sheep Man looks after it."

Yumiyoshi took the penlight from me and leafed through the pamphlet. I was casually observing my own shadow, wondering where the Sheep Man was, when I was suddenly struck by a horrifying realization: I'd let go of Yumiyoshi's hand!

My heart leapt into my throat. I was not ever to let go of her hand. I was fevered and swimming in sweat. I rushed to grab Yumiyoshi by the wrist. *If we don't let go, we'll be safe.* But it was already too late. At the very moment I extended my hand, her body was absorbed into the wall. Just like Kiki had passed through the wall of the death chamber. Just like quicksand. She was gone, she had disappeared, together with the glow of the penlight.

"Yumiyoshi!" I yelled.

No one answered. Silence and cold reigned, the darkness deepened.

"Yumiyoshi!" I yelled again.

"Hey, it's simple," came Yumiyoshi's voice from beyond the wall. "Really simple. You can pass right through the wall."

"No!" I screamed. "Don't be tricked. You think it's simple, but you'll never get back. It's different over there. That's the otherworld. It's not like here."

No answer came from her. Silence filled the room, pressing down as if I were on the ocean floor.

I was overwhelmed by my helplessness, despairing. Yumiyoshi was gone. After all this, I would never be able to reach her again. She was gone.

༄

There was no time to think. What was there to do? I loved her, I couldn't lose her. I followed her into the wall. I found myself passing through a transparent pocket of air.

It was cool as water. Time wavered, sequentiality twisted, gravity lost its force. Memories, old memories, like vapor, wafted up. The degeneration of my flesh accelerated. I passed through the huge, complex knot of my own DNA. The earth expanded, then chilled and contracted. Sheep were submerged in the cave. The sea was one enormous idea, rain falling silently over its vastness. Faceless people stood on the beachhead gazing out to the deep. An endless spool of time unraveled across the sky. A void enveloped the phantom figures and was encompassed by a yet greater void. Flesh melted to the bone and blew away like dust. *Extremely, irrevocably dead,* said someone. *Cuck-koo.* My body decomposed, blew apart—and was whole again.

I emerged through this layer of chaos, naked, in bed. It was dark, but not the lacquer-black darkness I feared. Still, I could not see. I reached out my hand. No one was beside me. I was alone, abandoned, at the edge of the world.

"Yumiyoshi!" I screamed at the top of my lungs. But no sound emerged, except for a dry rasping in my throat. I screamed again. And then I heard a tiny click.

The light had been switched on. Yumiyoshi smiled as she sat on the sofa in her blouse and skirt and shoes. Her light blue blazer was draped over the back of the chair. My hands were clutching the sheets. I slowly relaxed my fingers, feeling the tension drain from my body. I wiped the sweat from my face. I was back on this side. The light filling the room was real light.

"Yumiyoshi," I said hoarsely.

⚓

"Yes?"

"Are you really there?"

"Of course, I'm here."

"You didn't disappear?"

"No. People don't disappear so easily."

"It was a dream then."

"I know. I was here all the time, watching you. You were sleeping and dreaming and calling my name. I watched you in the dark. I could see you, you know."

I looked at the clock. A little before four, a little before dawn. The hour when thoughts are deepest. I was cold, my body was stiff. Then it was a dream? The Sheep Man gone, Yumiyoshi disappearing, the pain and despair. But I could remember the touch of Yumiyoshi's hand. The touch was still there within me. More real than this reality.

"Yumiyoshi?"

"Yes?"

"Why are you dressed?"

"I wanted to watch you with my clothes on," she said.

"Mind getting undressed again?" I asked. It was one way to be sure.

"Not at all," she said, removing her clothes and easing under the covers. She was warm and smooth, with the weight of someone real.

"I told you people don't just disappear," she said.

Oh really? I thought as I embraced her. No, anything can happen. This world is more fragile, more tenuous than we could ever know.

Who was skeleton number six then? The Sheep Man? Someone else? Myself? Waiting in that room so dim and distant. Far off, I heard the sound of the old Dolphin Hotel, like a train in the night. The *cr-cr-crr-creaking* of the elevator,

꘎

going up, up, stopping. Someone walking the halls, someone opening a door, someone closing a door. It was the old Dolphin. I could tell. Because I was part of it. And someone was crying for me. Crying for me because I couldn't cry.

I kissed Yumiyoshi on her eyelids.

She snuggled into the crook of my arm and fell asleep. But I couldn't sleep. It was impossible for my body to sleep. I was as wide awake as a dry well. I held Yumiyoshi tightly, and I cried. I cried inside. I cried for all that I'd lost and all that I'd lose. Yumiyoshi was soft as the ticking of time, her breath leaving a warm, damp spot on my arm. Reality.

Eventually dawn crept up on us. I watched the second hand on the alarm clock going around in real time. Little by little by little, onward.

I knew I would stay.

Seven o'clock came, and summer morning light eased through the window, casting a skewed rectangle on the floor.

"Yumiyoshi," I whispered. "It's morning."

SORROW AND REMORSE

✖

"A   WAKING"

A Mexican poet, essayist, and critic and winner of the 1990 Nobel
Prize for literature, Octavio Paz has written several volumes of
poetry since his first at the age of nineteen. His major prose work is
The Labyrinth of Solitude. "A Waking" *(Un despertar)* was originally
included in *A Sun More Alive (Un sol mas vivo).*

I was walled inside a dream.
Its walls had no consistency,
no weight: its emptiness was its weight.
The walls were hours and the hours
sorrow, hoarded forever.
The time of those hours was not time.

I leapt through a breach: in this world
it was four o'clock. The room was my room
and my ghost was in each thing.
I wasn't there. I looked out the window:
not a soul under the electric light.
Vigilant streetlamps, dirty snow,
houses and cars asleep, the insomnia
of a lamp, the oak that talks to itself,
the wind and its knives, the illegible
writing of the constellations.

The things were buried deep in themselves
and my eyes of flesh saw them
weary of being, realities
stripped of their names. My two eyes
were souls grieving for the world.
On the empty street the presence
passed without passing, vanishing
into its forms, fixed in its changes,
and turned now into houses, oaks, snow, time.
Life and death flowed on, blurred together.

Uninhabited sight, the presence
looked at me with nobody's eyes:
a bundle of reflections over the cliffs.
I looked inside: the room was my room
and I wasn't there. Being lacks nothing
—always full of itself, always the same—
even though we are not there . . . Outside,
the clarities, still uncertain:
dawn in the jumble of the rooftops.
The constellations were being erased.

KATHERINE MANSFIELD

✣

"MRS. NIGHTINGALE: A DREAM"

New Zealand–born short-story writer and poet Katherine Mansfield's (1888–1923) brief career and life—she died of tuberculosis at the age of thirty-four—were punctuated by her notable contributions to the modern short-story form. Employing a naturalistic approach to her subject, she often revealed subtle psychological elements of her characters' lives. Two elements of this dream sequence from the *Journal of Katherine Mansfield* touch on the disturbing conseqences of the author's life, chronic illness—the "many, many plural adhesions" refers to scars on her lungs from TB—and, reflecting the fact that Mansfield was never able to bear children, a vain search for a midwife.

*N*ovember. Walking up a dark hill with high iron fences at the sides of the road and immense trees over, I was looking for a midwife, Mrs. Nightingale. A little girl, barefoot, with a handkerchief over her head pattered up and put her chill hand in mine; she would lead me.

A light showed from a general shop. Inside a beautiful fair angry young woman directed me up the hill and to the right.

"You should have believed *me!*" said the child, and dug her nails into my palm.

There reared up a huge wall with a blank notice plastered on it. That was the house. In a low room, sitting by a table, a dirty yellow and black rug on her knees, an old hag sat. She had a grey handkerchief on her head. Beside her on the table

❈

was a jar of onions and a fork. I explained. She was to come to mother. Mother was very delicate: her eldest daughter was thirty-one and she had heart disease. "So please come at once."

"Has she any adhesions?" muttered the old hag, and she speared an onion, ate it and rubbed her nose.

"Oh, yes"—I put my hands on my breast—"many, many plural adhesions."

"Ah, that's bad, that's very bad," said the old crone, hunching up the rug so that through the fringe I saw her square slippers. "But I can't come. I've a case at four o'clock."

At that moment a healthy, bonny young woman came in with a bundle. She sat down by the midwife and explained, "Jinnie has had hers already." She unwound the bundle too quickly: a new-born baby with round eyes fell forward on her lap. I felt the pleasure of the little girl beside me—a kind of quiver. The young woman blushed and lowered her voice. "I got her to . . ." And she paused to find a very *medical private* word to describe washing. . . . "To *navigate* with a bottle of English water," she said, "but it isn't all away yet."

Mrs. Nightingale told me to go to the friend, Madame Léger, who lived on the terrace with a pink light before her house. I went. The terrace of houses was white and grey-blue in the moonlight with dark pines down the road. I saw the exquisite pink light. But just then there was a clanking sound behind me, and there was the little girl, bursting with breathlessness dragging in her arms a huge black bag. "Mrs. Nightingale says you forgot this."

So *I* was the midwife. I walked on thinking: "I'll go and have a look at the poor little soul. But it won't be for a long time yet."

VIRGINIA WOOLF

❧

Virginia Woolf (1882–1941), the English novelist, critic, and essayist, is best known for her innovative and occasionally experimental approach to fiction. Katherine Mansfield was a friend and literary rival of Woolf's for several years. There was no other woman writer at the time whom Woolf felt was worthy of vying for mastery in her field. In response to Mansfield's death in January, 1923, Virginia wrote: "Go on writing of course; but into emptiness. There's no competitor."

52 Tavistock Square, WC1
Saturday 7 July 1928

*A*ll last night I dreamt of Katherine Mansfield and wondered what dreams are; often evoke so much more than thinking does—almost as if she came back in person and was outside one, actively making one feel; instead of a figment called up and recollected, as she is, now, if I think of her. Yet some emotion lingers on the day after a dream; even though I've now almost forgotten what happened in the dream, except that she was lying on a sofa in a room high up, and a great many sad faced women were round her. Yet somehow I got the feel of her, and of her as if alive again, more than by day.

EDMUND WILSON

❧

from THE THIRTIES, THE FORTIES, and THE FIFTIES

An American literary and social critic, novelist, short-story writer, and poet, Edmund Wilson (1895–1972) incorporated many contemporary social, psychological, and political concepts into his writing. Wilson was regarded as an influential critic who played a large role in establishing the reputations of such writers as F. Scott Fitzgerald and John Dos Passos.

For several years, Wilson had recurring dreams about his second wife, Margaret Canby. Their brief (two-year), tumultuous marriage—both were notoriously heavy drinkers—had come to an abrupt conclusion when she died in a freak accident. Margaret, apparently having had a great deal to drink, died of a fracture to her skull after falling down a flight of stairs while attending a party in Santa Barbara. At the time, Wilson was with another woman on the East Coast, and the event had a devastating impact on his life. An overwhelming sense of guilt and remorse, which haunted him throughout much of his life, led him through a series of even more tumultuous episodes, including his subsequent marriage to author Mary McCarthy. In the five dream selections presented here Wilson reveals just how intensely he remains caught up in his conflicting feelings about Margaret twenty years after her death, even during his last marriage to Elena Thornton.

"NEW YORK, 53RD STREET,
1932–1933"

*D*ream. I was away with her in the country somewhere and she was getting more and more neurotic, and I realized I had better send her to McKinny (the psychiatrist I went to when I had my breakdown) so that the same thing wouldn't happen to her that had happened to Margaret —I was looking his number up in the telephone book.— Then I began to come to and had to face it that the woman in the dream was Margaret herself.

*D*ream. She was ill and supposed not to have long to live, lying on a bed somewhere we had gone to see a woman doctor—as we were talking, it occurred to me that she might get well, and if I could make her believe that I loved her and wanted her to get well, the trouble might disappear—I told her that she must get well, that she wasn't so seriously sick—she said she didn't know whether she was going to like what the doctor would tell her to do—I told her about my dreams, how I had thought we were back at the Berkeley, etc., and then waked up to find she was dead, but now she didn't need to die, there was time for me to convince her I wanted her to get well—yet I asked myself, were the other possibilities of getting some other more congenial, more intellectually developed woman able to tempt me? now that I could have her again, was the same doubt and negative feeling toward her that had kept us apart cropping up again? did I find now that I thought I could have her again that I wanted her less than I had in the dream in the Berkeley

❈

when I couldn't have her because she was dead? —I decided
I did want her, yes, and I could have her, and persuade her to
live. —Woke up among all the green foliage and lovely peace
of a slightly overcast June Sunday at Red Bank.

"BACK EAST"

*D*ream *about Margaret [Canby], mid-
January '47.* I had married someone else (not Elena) whom
I thought I liked very much, then I got a letter from her in
California. There she had been all the time and I hadn't realized, hadn't looked her up—I could have been back with her
and not have had to marry again. I would write to her right
away, but I couldn't undo my marriage—yet I was excited by
the prospect of seeing her, of talking to her again.

"ISRAEL AND THE DEAD SEA SCROLLS, 1952-1953"

*D*ream *about Margaret at Tel Aviv:*
I thought I had gone, in New York, to the apartment of some
California friend—it was only after a moment that I realized
that the woman there was Margaret, very attractive and still
young. We didn't communicate, the visit shifted. I had gone
home, wanted to find her again; searched in the phone book
under Canby and Waterman, then realized she would not be
there, would be just in from the Coast for a visit as she had

been when we first came together. I woke up as I was still trying to think how to reach her.

—What is the meaning of these still recurring dreams, in relation to my frequent dreams of alienations and separations from Elena? In these latter, it is not merely a question of fears, but also of the desire to assert my independence—yet the two are bound up together. My impulse to free myself from relationships with women had something to do with my letting Margaret go off to Santa Barbara, where she died. Now in dreams I want her back. I have Elena but dream of leaving her.

"WELLFLEET AND NEW YORK, 1955-1956"

*N*ightmare: My horrible nightmare at the beginning of April—the worst I have had since the little blue light. I thought that I was back—alone, at night—in the old house at Red Bank (which I dream about constantly, near the one Mother bought after Father's death), with the corpses of two people I had killed. I propped them up at the dining-room table in the walnut-stained paneled dining room. I had turned off the lights, and the room was pitch-dark, and I lay back, a little way from the table, in the kind of chair in which one reclines. The body of the woman was facing me—I was vague about the other, a man. I thought, "This is Hell—can I stand it? A bottle of whisky might help—but how horrible to make oneself indifferent and cheerful in order to dull oneself to a thing like this!" But I decided I couldn't stand it and got up and made my way through the dark house.

❧

I was thinking on the way that there *was* a bottle—almost untouched—of whisky, and that I could always depend on that, could come back and drink it. I went out the front door and down the steps to the lawn; but I had hardly stepped off the bottom step when my mother appeared from behind me and stopped me. My state of mind then became that of a child. She led me back into the house, and into the dining room. She turned on the lights, and there was nothing there. I remembered that I had not, after all, left the bodies propped up at the table: I had decided to put them away. My mother went over to the cupboard under the left corner china closet —where she used to hide candy and cakes—and opened it. Inside there were simply large puppets of mine that I had put away, laying them on their sides. What I had thought was the corpse of a woman was simply a puppet-queen.

I think that the woman was Margaret and the male body my father (who was not in the house in the dream). I have felt guilty in connection with the deaths of both.

PHILIP LARKIN

✖

"WHY DID I DREAM OF YOU LAST NIGHT?"

In addition to two novels, English poet and novelist Philip Larkin (1922–1985) published only four short volumes of verse during his lifetime. After his death, these were assembled in *Collected Poems*. Less radical in his stylistic approach to poetry than several of his contemporaries, Larkin, through his verse, established himself as a leader in the English antiromantic movement. Though often witty and colloquial in tone, his poetry contemplates a more melancholy, elegiac view of life.

*W*hy did I dream of you last night?
  Now morning is pushing back hair with grey light
  Memories strike home, like slaps in the face:
Raised on elbow, I stare at the pale fog
        beyond the window.

  So many things I had thought forgotten
  Return to my mind with stranger pain:
—Like letters that arrive addressed to someone
Who left the house so many years ago.

1939

❧

"I DREAMED OF AN OUT-THRUST ARM OF LAND"

I dreamed of an out-thrust arm of land
Where gulls blew over a wave
That fell along miles of sand;
And the wind climbed up the caves
To tear at a dark-faced garden
Whose black flowers were dead,
And broke round a house we slept in,
A drawn blind and a bed.

I was sleeping, and you woke me
To walk on the chilled shore
Of a night with no memory,
Till your voice forsook my ear
Till your two hands withdrew
And I was empty of tears,
On the edge of a bricked and streeted sea
And a cold hill of stars.

Arabesque, Hilary term 1943, TNS

WILLIAM TREVOR

❦

from FELICIA'S JOURNEY

William Trevor's novels include *The Children of Dynmouth* and *Fools of Fortune.* The Irish writer's eight volumes of short stories were brought together in *The Collected Stories* in 1992. *Felicia's Journey* focuses on a young woman's flight from her home in Ireland. As she scours the countryside in a vain search for the father of her unborn child, a series of tragic events transpire that eventually lead to her being coerced into aborting her child. In the brilliantly revealing dream sequence, occurring during the aftermath of this event, Trevor captures in a few short paragraphs the stream of attitudes and ideas that have shaped this woman's life.

She is warm beneath the bedclothes, safe in the bed with the wide mahogany bedstead and carved headboard that almost fills the room, one of its sides pressed against pink flowered wallpaper. A single window is a yard from its foot, and there's a mat to step out on to, the only covering on the stained floorboards. There are plain blue curtains, which she has never drawn back, through which light filters in the daytime. Three heavily framed pictures are murky on the other walls, scenes of military action. The room contains neither a wardrobe nor a chest of drawers.

She is aware of the pain that lingers, worse than it was, and the bleeding that lingers also, and of tiredness. Again her eyelids droop and she drifts away, her body seeming strangely elongated as she lies there, her feet so far away they might not be there at all, a numbness somewhere else. On the Creagh road a car going by sounds its horn; Johnny waves because it's someone he knows, and then they turn off into the Mandeville woods. People are made for one another, he murmurs, his lips kissing her hair and her neck. His grey-green eyes are lit up because they're together again, because all the looking for him is over. "Will I put the potato stack on the top of it?" Miss Furey's brother asks, and points at the hole he has dug in the corner of the field, beyond the yard. "Would we do it at night?" he asks. "Only someone might come into the yard. If it was daytime we'd have to think of that." The corpse is under the hay in the barn. She carries it to the field, following him in the darkness and laying it down in the pit, the small amount of skin and blood that remains already disintegrating. "It's the only way," someone says, and clay is shovelled in, the sods put back.

She begs for forgiveness, clutching at the robes of the Virgin. But the eyes of the Virgin are blind, without whites or pupils, and then the statue falls down from the dresser and is gone for ever also. "Oh, aren't you terrible, Felicia!" The Reverend Mother is cross, sweeping the pieces into a dustpan. And her own mother is shelling peas in the doorway, the door open to the yard, and tears fall on to the peas in the colander. "Supposing I'd done that to you, Felicia," is what her mother tries to say, speaking made difficult because of her sobbing. But Felicia knows anyway. She knows what the words are even though they aren't spoken.

IDENTITY AND DISCOVERY

REYNOLDS PRICE

❈

"WASHED FEET"

An American novelist and short-story writer, Reynolds Price set his work firmly in his native North Carolina. His novels include *A Long and Happy Life*, *The Source of Light*, and *Kate Vaiden*. "Washed Feet" is the fourth in a series of five connecting stories entitled "Good and Bad Dreams," featured in *The Collected Stories*, published in 1993.

*H*e has slept this soundly since four in the morning because when he came back, his mind was clear. It knew only one thing—the doctor's words on leaving her ward, "She can live if she wants; we've done that much." (They had, the doctor and his nameless team, had worked four hours repairing her, patiently ligating all she'd severed— the brachial artery and vein—anastomosing tendons, pumping in the mandatory blood that would be at least no stranger to her than the pints she'd carefully drained tonight; then had wheeled her still unconscious to a lighted ward and watched her like a bomb.) The words had instantly swelled in his head, a polished plug molded to crowd his skull and exclude all else, every atom of air. And had perfectly succeeded. He had come here—a half-hour walk, a taxi—had lit the gas-fire (no other light), then stripped and slept. No question of why or who was at fault—"The woman with whom I have lived six years has tried to kill herself. A serious try—no skittish theatrics. I found her; they saved her; she can live if she wants." No question of how.

❦

Two hours of dreamless sleep. It is six, but still winter dark; only the low red burn of the gas—he is sleeping his own way, in warmth.

This happens. A man is in the room, standing darkly in a corner. In his sleep, he sees the man and does not feel fear or curiosity; only watches till he knows what's required of him—that he thrust with his bare feet till they've cleared sheets and blankets and lie exposed. That is the necessary sign. The man moves forward to the end of the bed; stands waiting, still dark. No question of seeing his face or dress. He is dark. No need to know—only lie there flat on your back and wait. Now the man is looking round the room— he is needing something. Lie still, he will find it. And the man goes on looking, even moves a few steps in various directions. Is his face distraught?—lie still, don't wonder, he can fill his own needs. In calm desperation, the man returns to his place at the end of the bed; kneels suddenly. He silently spits in the palms of both hands and washes the bare feet propped before him. The gestures are gentle but the palms are rough.

He is scrubbed awake. He lies on his back, his feet are uncovered, they sweat though the room is hardly warm. He raises his head to see the room. Empty of all but red gas light and the customary stuffing, their stifling freight. He knows he was dreaming. No man is here. No one but himself.

Yet he also knows (he falls back for this) another new thing, more filling than the last—that from now (this night, this momentary dream) he must walk in his life as though a man had been here—one who had come precisely here by choice and desperate to forgive, had searched for water, then knelt and washed his feet (till then unjudged) with the agent available—His spit, that wishes to clean but scalds.

from THE ENIGMA OF ARRIVAL

Born in Trinidad and raised in a Hindu family, V. S. Naipaul went to
England on a scholarship in 1950. He began writing after spending
four years at Oxford, eventually settling in London. He has written
over twenty volumes of essays and fiction, including *A House for
Mr. Biswas, A Bend in the River,* and *A Way in the World: A Novel.*
His autobiographical novel, *The Enigma of Arrival,* centers on
Naipaul's experience of being a West Indian exile living in England.

*T*o write about Jack and his cottage and
his garden it was necessary for me to have lived a second
life in the valley and to have had a second awakening to the
natural world there. But a version of that story—a version—
came to me just days after I came to the valley, to the cottage
in the manor grounds.

The cottage at that time still had the books and some
of the furniture of the people who had been there before.
Among the books was one that was very small, a paperback
booklet, smaller in format than the average small paperback
and with only a few pages. The booklet, from a series called
the Little Library of Art, was about the early paintings of
Giorgio de Chirico. There were about a dozen reproductions
of his early surrealist paintings. Technically, in these very
small reproductions, the paintings did not seem interesting;
they seemed flat, facile. And their content was not profound
either: arbitrary assemblages, in semi-classical, semi-modern
settings, of unrelated motifs—aqueducts, trains, arcades,

gloves, fruit, statues—with an occasional applied touch of easy mystery: in one painting, for instance, an overlarge shadow of a hidden figure approaching from round a corner.

But among these paintings there was one which, perhaps because of its title, caught my attention: *The Enigma of Arrival.* I felt that in an indirect, poetical way the title referred to something in my own experience; and later I was to learn that the titles of these surrealist paintings of Chirico's hadn't been given by the painter, but by the poet Apollinaire, who died young in 1918, from influenza following a war wound, to the great grief of Picasso and others.

What was interesting about the painting itself, *The Enigma of Arrival,* was that—again perhaps because of the title—it changed in my memory. The original (or the reproduction in the Little Library of Art booklet) was always a surprise. A classical scene, Mediterranean, ancient-Roman— or so I saw it. A wharf; in the background, beyond walls and gateways (like cutouts), there is the top of the mast of an antique vessel; on an otherwise deserted street in the foreground there are two figures, both muffled, one perhaps the person who has arrived, the other perhaps a native of the port. The scene is of desolation and mystery: it speaks of the mystery of arrival. It spoke to me of that, as it had spoken to Apollinaire.

And in the winter gray of the manor grounds in Wiltshire, in those first four days of mist and rain, when so little was clear to me, an idea—floating lightly above the book I was working on—came to me of a story I might one day write about that scene in the Chirico picture.

My story was to be set in classical times, in the Mediterranean. My narrator would write plainly, without any attempt at period style or historical explanation of his period. He would arrive—for a reason I had yet to work out—at that classical port with the walls and gateways like cutouts. He would walk past that muffled figure on the quayside. He would move from that silence and desolation, that blankness, to a gateway or door. He would enter there and be swallowed by the life and noise of a crowded city (I imagined something like an Indian bazaar scene). The mission he had come on—family business, study, religious initiation—would give him encounters and adventures. He would enter interiors, of houses and temples. Gradually there would come to him a feeling that he was getting nowhere; he would lose his sense of mission; he would begin to know only that he was lost. His feeling of adventure would give way to panic. He would want to escape, to get back to the quayside and his ship. But he wouldn't know how. I imagined some religious ritual in which, led on by kindly people, we would unwittingly take part and find himself the intended victim. At the moment of crisis he would come upon a door, open it, and find himself back on the quayside of arrival. He has been saved; the world is as he remembered it. Only one thing is missing now. Above the cutout walls and buildings there is no mast, no sail. The antique ship has gone. The traveler has lived out his life.

I didn't think of this as an historical story, but more as a free ride of the imagination. There was to be no research. I would take pointers from Virgil perhaps for the sea and travel and the seasons, from the Gospels and the Acts of the Apostles for the feel of the municipal or provincial organization of the Roman Empire; I would get moods and the idea of ancient religion from Apuleius; Horace and Martial and Petronius would give me hints for social settings.

The idea of living in my imagination in that classical Roman world was attractive to me. A beautiful, clear, dangerous world, far removed from the setting in which I had found myself; the story, more a mood than a story, so different from

❧

the book on which I was working. A taxing book: it had been occupying me for eight or nine months and I still hadn't completed a draft.

At the center of the book I was writing was a story set in an African country, once a colony, with white and Asian settlers, and now independent. It was the story of a day-long journey made in a car by two white people at the time of tribal war, suddenly coming, suddenly overwhelming colonial order and simplicity. Africa had given both those white people a chance, made them bigger, brought out their potential; now, when they were no longer so young, it was consuming them. It was a violent book—not violent in its incidents, but in its emotions.

It was a book about fear. All the jokes were silenced by this fear. And the mist that hung over the valley where I was writing; the darkness that came early; the absence of knowledge of where I was—all this uncertainty emanating from the valley I transferred to my Africa. And it did not occur to me that the story of *The Enigma of Arrival*—a sunlit sea journey ending in a dangerous classical city—which had come to me as a kind of release from the creative rigors and the darkness of my own African story, it did not occur to me that that Mediterranean story was really no more than a version of the story I was already writing.

Nor did it occur to me that it was also an attempt to find a story for, to give coherence to, a dream or nightmare which for a year or so had been unsettling me. In this dream there occurred always, at a critical moment in the dream narrative, what I can only describe as an explosion in my head. It was how every dream ended, with this explosion that threw me flat on my back, in the presence of people, in a street, a crowded room, or wherever, threw me into this degraded posture in the midst of standing people, threw me into the posture of sleep in which I found myself when I awakened. The explosion was so loud, so reverberating and slow in my head that I felt, with the part of my brain that miraculously could still think and draw conclusions, that I couldn't possibly survive, that I was in fact dying, that the explosion this time, in this dream, regardless of the other dreams that had revealed themselves at the end as dreams, would kill, that I was consciously living through, or witnessing, my own death. And when I awoke my head felt queer, shaken up, exhausted; as though some discharge in my brain had in fact occurred.

This dream or nightmare or internal dramatization—perhaps a momentary turbulence in my brain had created the split-second tableau of the street, the café, the party, the bus, where I collapsed in the presence of people—had been with me for a year or more. It was a dream that had been brought on by intellectual fatigue and something like grief.

I had written a lot, done work of much difficulty; had worked under pressure more or less since my schooldays. Before the writing, there had been the learning; writing had come to me slowly. Before that, there had been Oxford; and before that, the school in Trinidad where I had worked for the Oxford scholarship. There had been a long preparation for the writing career! And then I discovered that to be a writer was not (as I had imagined) a state—of competence, or achievement, or fame, or content—at which one arrived and where one stayed. There was a special anguish attached to the career: whatever the labor of any piece of writing, whatever its creative challenges and satisfactions, time had always taken me away from it. And, with time passing, I felt mocked by what I had already done; it seemed to belong to a time of vigor, now past for good. Emptiness, restlessness built up again; and it was necessary once more, out of my internal

resources alone, to start on another book, to commit myself
to that consuming process again.

I had finally been undermined. My spirit had broken;
and that breaking of the spirit had occurred not long before
I had come to the valley. For two years I had worked on an
historical book about the region where I had been born. The
book had grown; and since (beyond a certain length) a big
book is harder to write, more exhausting, than a shorter one,
I had resisted its growth. But then I had become excited by
the story it told. The historian seeks to abstract principles
from human events. My approach was the other; for the two
years that I lived among the documents I sought to recon-
struct the human story as best I could.

It was a labor. Ten or twelve documents—called up from
memory, almost like personal memories—might provide the
details for a fairly short and simple paragraph of narrative.
But I was supported by my story, the themes it touched on:
discovery, the New World, the dispeopling of the discovered
islands; slavery, the creation of the plantation colony; the
coming of the idea of revolution; the chaos after revolutions
in societies so created.

A great packed education those two years had been. And
I had such faith in what I was writing, such faith in the
grandeur of my story, that I thought it would find the readers that my books of the previous twelve years had not found.
And I behaved foolishly. Without waiting for that response,
I dismantled the little life I had created for myself in England
and prepared to leave, to be a free man.

For years, in that far-off island whose human history
I had been discovering and writing about, I had dreamed of
coming to England. But my life in England had been savor-
less, and much of it mean. I had taken to England all the raw-
ness of my colonial's nerves, and those nerves had more or

less remained, nerves which in the beginning were in a good part also the nerves of youth and inexperience, physical and sexual inadequacy, and of undeveloped talent. And just as once at home I had dreamed of being in England, so for years in England I had dreamed of leaving England. Now, eighteen years after my first arrival, it seemed to me that the time had come. I dismantled the life I had bit by bit established, and prepared to go. The house I had bought and renovated in stages I sold; and my furniture and books and papers went to the warehouse.

The calamity occurred four months later. The book in which I had placed such faith, the book which had exhausted me so much, could not please the publisher who had commissioned it. We had misunderstood one another. He knew only my name; he did not know the nature of my work. And I had misunderstood his interest in me. He had approached me as a serious writer, but he had wanted only a book for tourists, something much simpler than the book I had written; something at once more romantic and less romantic; at once more human and less human. So I found myself up in the air. And I had to return to England.

That journey back—from the island and continent I had gone to see with my new vision, the corner of the New World I had just written about, from there to the United States and Canada, and then to England—that journey back to England so mimicked and parodied the journey of nineteen years before, the journey of the young man, the boy almost, who had journeyed to England to be a writer, in a country where the calling had some meaning, that I couldn't but be aware of all the cruel ironies.

It was out of this grief, too deep for tears or rage—grief that began partly to be expressed in the dream of the exploding head—that I began to write my African story, which had come to me as a wisp of an idea in Africa three or four years before.

The African fear with which as a writer I was living day after day; the unknown Wiltshire; the cruelty of this return to England, the dread of a second failure; the mental fatigue. All of this, rolled into one, was what lay on the spirit of the man who went on the walks down to Jack's cottage and past it. Not an observer merely, a man removed; but a man played on, worked on, by many things.

And it was out of that burden of emotion that there had come to the writer, as release, as an idyll, the ship story, the antique quayside story, suggested by *The Enigma of Arrival;* an idea that came innocently, without the writer's suspecting how much of his life, how many aspects of his life, that remote story (still just an idea for a story) carried. But that is why certain stories or incidents suggest themselves to writers, or make an impression on them; that is why writers can appear to have obsessions.

I went for my walks every afternoon. I finished my book. The panic of its composition didn't repeat in the revision. I was beginning to heal. And more than heal. For me, a miracle had occurred in this valley and in the grounds of the manor where my cottage was. In that unlikely setting, in the ancient heart of England, a place where I was truly an alien, I found I was given a second chance, a new life, richer and fuller than any I had had anywhere else. And in that place, where at the beginning I had looked only for remoteness and a place to hide, I did some of my best work. I traveled; I wrote. I ventured out, brought back experiences to my cottage; and wrote. The years passed. I healed. The life around me changed. I changed.

And then one afternoon came that choking fit as I was walking past Jack's old cottage—Jack himself long dead.

A few hours later came the serious illness which that choking fit had presaged. And when after some months I recovered, I found myself a middle-aged man. Work became harder for me. I discovered in myself an unwillingness to undertake new labor; I wished to be free of labor.

And whereas when I came to the valley my dream was the dream provoked by fatigue and unhappiness—the dream of the exploding head, the certainty of death—now it was the idea of death itself that came to me in my sleep. Death not as a tableau or a story, as in the earlier dream; but death, the end of things, as a gloom that got at a man, sought out his heart, when he was at his weakest, while he slept. This idea of death, death the nullifier of human life and endeavor, to which morning after morning I awakened, so enervated me that it sometimes took me all day, all the hours of daylight, to see the world as real again, to become a man again, a doer.

The dream of exhaustion once; now the debilitation brought on by involuntary thoughts of the final emptiness. This too was something that happened to the man who went walking, witness of people and events in the valley.

It was as though the calling, the writer's vocation, was one that could never offer me anything but momentary fulfillment. So that again, years after I had seen the Chirico picture and the idea for the story had come to me, again, in my own life, was another version of the story of *The Enigma of Arrival.*

DORIS LESSING

✇

from THE GOLDEN NOTEBOOK

Born in Persia and for many years a resident of southern Rhodesia, English fiction writer Doris Lessing is one of the great visionary novelists of our time. Her work ranges from the social realism of novels like *Martha Quest* and *The Four-Gated City* to her psychological observations of madness and neurosis in *Briefing for a Descent into Hell* and *The Summer Before the Dark* to the futuristic, six-novel series *Canopus in Argus: Archives.* Her most famous work, however, remains *The Golden Notebook,* a hugely ambitious experimental novel that incorporates several different journal forms into a carefully structured story. Lessing brings power and resonance to her dream sequences, and the dream excerpted here vividly brings a level of depth and awareness to the development of this character's life.

23rd April

I had a dream for my last appointment. I took it to Mrs Marks. I dreamed I held a kind of casket in my hands, and inside it was something very previous. I was walking up a long room, like an art gallery or a lecture hall, full of dead pictures and statues. (When I used the word dead, Mrs Marks smiled, ironically.) There was a small crowd of people waiting at the end of the hall on a kind of platform. They were waiting for me to hand them the casket. I was incredibly happy that at last I could give them this precious object. But when I handed it over, I saw suddenly they were

all businessmen, brokers, something like that. They did not
open the box, but started handing me large sums of money.
I began to cry. I shouted: 'Open the box, open the box,' but
they couldn't hear me, or wouldn't listen. Suddenly I saw
they were all characters in some film or play, and that I had
written it, and was ashamed of it. It all turned into farce,
flickering and grotesque, I was a character in my own play.
I opened the box and forced them to look. But instead of a
beautiful thing, which I thought would be there, there was
a mass of fragments, and pieces. Not a whole thing, broken
into fragments, but bits and pieces from everywhere, all over
the world—I recognised a lump of red earth that I knew
came from Africa, and then a bit of metal that came off a gun
from Indo-China, and then everything was horrible, bits of
flesh from people killed in the Korean War and a communist
party badge off someone who died in a Soviet prison. This,
looking at the mass of ugly fragments, was so painful that
I couldn't look, and I shut the box. But the group of businessmen or money-people hadn't noticed. They took the box
from me and opened it. I turned away so as not to see, but
they were delighted. At last I looked and I saw that there was
something in the box. It was a small green crocodile with
a winking sardonic snout. I thought it was the image of a
crocodile, made of jade, or emeralds, then I saw it was alive,
for large frozen tears rolled down its cheeks and turned
into diamonds. I laughed out loud when I saw how I had
cheated the businessmen and I woke up. Mrs Marks listened
to this dream without comment, she seemed uninterested.
We said good-bye with affection, but she has already turned
away, inwardly, as I have. She said I must 'drop in to see her'
if I needed her. I thought, how can I need you when you
have bequeathed to me your image; I know perfectly well
I shall dream of that large maternal witch every time I am in

❦

trouble. (Mrs Marks is a very small wiry, energetic woman, yet I have always dreamed of her as large and powerful.) I went out of that darkened, solemn room in which I have spent so many hours half-in, half-out, of fantasy and dream, the room which is like a shrine to art, and I reached the cold ugly pavement. I saw myself in a shop window: a small, rather pale, dry, spiky woman, and there was a wry look on my face which I recognised as the grin on the snout of that malicious little green crocodile in the crystal casket of my dream.

C . G . J U N G

✣

"CONFRONTATION WITH THE UNCONSCIOUS"

Carl Jung (1875–1961), the Swiss analytical psychologist, was influenced by Sigmund Freud's work in the analysis of dream content
early in his career. The two worked in close association for a few
years, but Jung broke with his colleague to develop his own concepts. He broadened Freud's definition of the libido to encompass
the totality of life's experiences and formulated his theory of the
collective unconscious. According to this theory, universal or time-
less elements of human experience are often expressed through
dreams, fantasies, and myths in the form of archetypal images nd
symbols. His concept of archetypal symbols was the basis of
his pioneering study *Man and His Symbols.* The excerpt here was
originally published in Jung's autobiographical work, *Memories,
Dreams, Reflections.*

*A*fter the parting of the ways with Freud,
a period of inner uncertainty began for me. It would be no
exaggeration to call it a state of disorientation. I felt totally
suspended in mid-air, for I had not yet found my own footing. Above all, I felt it necessary to develop a new attitude
toward my patients. I resolved for the present not to bring any
theoretical premises to bear upon them, but to wait and see
what they would tell of their own accord. My aim became to
leave things to chance. The result was that the patients would
spontaneously report their dreams and fantasies to me, and
I would merely ask, "What occurs to you in connection with

that?" or, "How do you mean that, where does that come from, what do you think about it?" The interpretations seemed to follow of their own accord from the patients' replies and associations. I avoided all theoretical points of view and simply helped the patients to understand the dream-images by themselves, without application of rules and theories.

Soon I realized that it was right to take the dreams in this way as the basis of interpretation, for that is how dreams are intended. They are the facts from which we must proceed. Naturally, the aspects resulting from this method were so multitudinous that the need for a criterion grew more and more pressing—the need, I might almost put it, for some initial orientation.

About this time I experienced a moment of unusual clarity in which I looked back over the way I had traveled so far. I thought, "Now you possess a key to mythology and are free to unlock all the gates of the unconscious psyche." But then something whispered within me, "Why open all gates?" And promptly the question arose of what, after all, I had accomplished. I had explained the myths of peoples of the past; I had written a book about the hero, the myth in which man has always lived. But in what myth does man live nowadays? In the Christian myth, the answer might be, "Do *you* live in it?" I asked myself. To be honest, the answer was no. For me, it is not what I live by. "Then do we no longer have any myth?" "No, evidently we no longer have any myth." "But then what is your myth—the myth in which you do live?" At this point the dialogue with myself became uncomfortable, and I stopped thinking. I had reached a dead end.

Then, around Christmas of 1912, I had a dream. In the dream I found myself in a magnificent Italian loggia with pillars, a marble floor, and a marble balustrade. I was sitting on a gold Renaissance chair; in front of me was a table of rare beauty. It was made of green stone, like emerald. There I sat, looking out into the distance, for the loggia was set high up on the tower of a castle. My children were sitting at the table too.

Suddenly a white bird descended, a small sea gull or a dove. Gracefully, it came to rest on the table, and I signed to the children to be still so that they would not frighten away the pretty white bird. Immediately, the dove was transformed into a little girl, about eight years of age, with golden blond hair. She ran off with the children and played with them among the colonnades of the castle.

I remained lost in thought, musing about what I had just experienced. The little girl returned and tenderly placed her arms around my neck. Then she suddenly vanished; the dove was back and spoke slowly in a human voice. "Only in the first hours of the night can I transform myself into a human being, while the male dove is busy with the twelve dead." Then she flew off into the blue air, and I awoke.

I was greatly stirred. What business would a male dove be having with twelve dead people? In connection with the emerald table the story of the Tabula Smaragdina occurred to me, the emerald table in the alchemical legend of Hermes Trismegistos. He was said to have left behind him a table upon which the basic tenets of alchemical wisdom were engraved in Greek.

I also thought of the twelve apostles, the twelve months of the year, the signs of the zodiac, etc. But I could find no solution to the enigma. Finally I had to give it up. All I knew with any certainty was that the dream indicated an unusual activation of the unconscious. But I knew no technique whereby I might get to the bottom of my inner processes, and so there

꘎

remained nothing for me to do but wait, go on with my life, and pay close attention to my fantasies.

One fantasy kept returning: there was something dead present, but it was also still alive. For example, corpses were placed in crematory ovens, but were then discovered to be still living. These fantasies came to a head and were simultaneously resolved in a dream.

I was in a region like the Alyscamps near Arles. There they have a lane of sarcophagi which go back to Merovingian times. In the dream I was coming from the city, and saw before me a similar lane with a long row of tombs. They were pedestals with stone slabs on which the dead lay. They reminded me of old church burial vaults, where knights in armor lie outstretched. Thus the dead lay in my dream, in their antique clothes, with hands clasped, the difference being that they were not hewn out of stone, but in a curious fashion mummified. I stood still in front of the first grave and looked at the dead man, who was a person of the eighteen-thirties. I looked at his clothes with interest, whereupon he suddenly moved and came to life. He unclasped his hands; but that was only because I was looking at him. I had an extremely unpleasant feeling, but walked on and came to another body. He belonged to the eighteenth century. There exactly the same thing happened: when I looked at him, he came to life and moved his hands. So I went down the whole row, until I came to the twelfth century—that is, to a crusader in chain mail who lay there with clasped hands. His figure seemed carved out of wood. For a long time I looked at him and thought he was really dead. But suddenly I saw that a finger of his left hand was beginning to stir gently.

Of course I had originally held to Freud's view that vestiges of old experiences exist in the unconscious. But dreams like this, and my actual experiences of the unconscious, taught me that such contents are not dead, outmoded forms, but belong to our living being. My work had confirmed this assumption, and in the course of years there developed from it the theory of archetypes.

The dreams, however, could not help me over my feeling of disorientation. On the contrary, I lived as if under constant inner pressure. At times this became so strong that I suspected there was some psychic disturbance in myself. Therefore I twice went over all the details of my entire life, with particular attention to childhood memories; for I thought there might be something in my past which I could not see and which might possibly be the cause of the disturbance. But this retrospection led to nothing but a fresh acknowledgment of my own ignorance. Thereupon I said to myself, "Since I know nothing at all, I shall simply do whatever occurs to me." Thus I consciously submitted myself to the impulses of the unconscious.

The first thing that came to the surface was a childhood memory from perhaps my tenth or eleventh year. At that time I had had a spell of playing passionately with building blocks. I distinctly recalled how I had built little houses and castles, using bottles to form the sides of gates and vaults. Somewhat later I had used ordinary stones, with mud for mortar. These structures had fascinated me for a long time. To my astonishment, this memory was accompanied by a good deal of emotion. "Aha," I said to myself, "there is still life in these things. The small boy is still around, and possesses a creative life which I lack. But how can I make my way to it?" For as a grown man it seemed impossible to me that I should be able to bridge the distance from the present back to my eleventh year. Yet if I wanted to re-establish contact with that period, I had no choice but to return to it and take up once more that

child's life with his childish games. This moment was a turning point in my fate, but I gave in only after endless resis-
tances and with a sense of resignation. For it was a painfully
humiliating experience to realize that there was nothing to be
done except play childish games.

Nevertheless, I began accumulating suitable stones,
gathering them partly from the lake shore and partly from
the water. And I started building: cottages, a castle, a whole
village. The church was still missing, so I made a square
building with a hexagonal drum on top of it, and a dome.
A church also requires an altar, but I hesitated to build that.

Preoccupied with the question of how I could approach
this task, I was walking along the lake as usual one day, picking stones out of the gravel on the shore. Suddenly I caught
sight of a red stone, a four-sided pyramid about an inch
and a half high. It was a fragment of stone which had been
polished into this shape by the action of the water—a pure
product of chance. I knew at once: this was the altar! I placed
it in the middle under the dome, and as I did so, I recalled the
underground phallus of my childhood dream. This connection gave me a feeling of satisfaction.

I went on with my building game after the noon meal
every day, whenever the weather permitted. As soon as I was
through eating, I began playing, and continued to do so until
the patients arrived; and if I was finished with my work early
enough in the evening, I went back to building. In the course
of this activity my thoughts clarified, and I was able to grasp
the fantasies whose presence in myself I dimly felt.

Naturally, I thought about the significance of what I was
doing, and asked myself, "Now, really, what are you about?
You are building a small town, and doing it as if it were a
rite!" I had no answer to my question, only the inner certainty
that I was on the way to discovering my own myth. For the

building game was only a beginning. It released a stream of fantasies which I later carefully wrote down.

This sort of thing has been consistent with me, and at any time in my later life when I came up against a blank wall, I painted a picture or hewed stone. Each such experience proved to be a *rite d'entrée* for the ideas and works that followed hard upon it. Everything that I have written this year and last year, "The Undiscovered Self," "Flying Saucers: A Modern Myth," "A Psychological View of Conscience," has grown out of the stone sculptures I did after my wife's death. The close of her life, the end, and what it made me realize, wrenched me violently out of myself. It cost me a great deal to regain my footing, and contact with stone helped me.

PAT BARKER

✖

from REGENERATION

British novelist Pat Barker originally focused her writing on the working-class milieu of her native northeast England, but in 1991 she shifted her attention to World War I with *Regeneration*. This novel, along with *The Eye in the Door* and the 1995 Booker Prize–winning *The Ghost Road*, form a trilogy that realistically depicts the fiercely emotional consequences of the war on soldiers and officers. Several historical characters are integrated into these novels, including the psychologist William Rivers, who specialized in treating victims of shell shock. His analysis of several of his patients' dreams is recreated with fascinating detail throughout the trilogy, and Barker brilliantly creates a context for the early science of analysis through her depiction of his approach.

I was walking up the drive at home. My wife was on the lawn having tea with some other ladies, they were all wearing white. As I got closer, my wife stood up and smiled and waved and then her expression changed and all the other ladies began to look at each other. I couldn't understand why, and then I looked down and saw that I was naked."

"What had you been wearing?"

"Uniform. When I saw how frightened they were, it made *me* frightened. I started to run and I was running through bushes. I was being chased by my father-in-law and two orderlies. Eventually they got me cornered and my father-in-law came towards me, waving a big stick. It had a snake wound round it. He was using it as a kind of flail, and the

⚓

snake was hissing. I backed away, but they got hold of me and tied me up."

Rivers detected a slight hesitation. "What with?"

A pause. In determinedly casual tones Anderson said, "A pair of lady's corsets. They fastened them round my arms and tied the laces."

"Like a strait-waistcoat?"

"Yes."

"Then?"

"Then I was carted off to some kind of carriage. I was thrown inside and the doors banged shut and it was very dark. Like a grave. The first time I looked it was empty, but then the next time you were there. You were wearing a post-mortem apron and gloves."

It was obvious from his tone that he'd finished. Rivers smiled and said, "It's a long time since I've worn those."

"I haven't recently worn corsets."

"Whose corsets were they?"

"Just corsets. You want me to say my wife's, don't you?"

Rivers was taken back. "I want you to say—"

"Well, I really don't think they were. I suppose it is *possible* someone might find being locked up in a loony bin a fairly *emasculating* experience?"

"I think most people do." Though not many said so. "I want you to say what you think."

No response.

"You say you woke up vomiting?"

"Yes."

"I wonder why? I mean I can quite see the sight of me in a post-mortem apron might not be to everybody's taste—"

"I don't know."

"What was the most frightening thing about the dream?"

"The snake."

A long silence.

"Do you often dream about snakes?"

"Yes."

Another long silence. "Well, go on, then," Anderson exploded at last. "That's what you Freudian Johnnies are on about all the time, isn't it? Nudity, snakes, *corsets*. You might at least try to look *grateful*, Rivers. It's a gift."

"I think if I'd made any association at all with the snake—and after all what possible relevance can my associations have?—it was probably with the one that's crawling up your lapel."

Anderson looked down at the caduceus badge of the RAMC which he wore on his tunic, and then across at the same badge on Rivers's tunic.

"What the er snake *might* suggest is that medicine is an issue between yourself and your father-in-law?"

"No."

"Not at all?"

"No."

Another long silence. Anderson said, "It depends what you mean by an issue."

"A subject on which there is habitual disagreement."

"No. Naturally my time in France has left me with a certain level of distaste for the practice of medicine, but that'll go in time. There's no *issue*. I have a wife and child to support."

"You're how old?"

"Thirty-six."

"And your little boy?"

Anderson's expression softened. "Five."

"School fees coming up?"

"Yes. I'll be all right once I've had a rest. Basically, I'm paying for last summer. Do you know, at one point we *averaged* ten amputations a day? Every time I was due for leave it was cancelled." He looked straight at Rivers. "There's no doubt what the problem is. Tiredness."

"I still find the vomiting puzzling. Especially since you say you feel no more than a *mild* disinclination for medicine."

"I didn't say mild, I said temporary."

"Ah. What in particular do you find difficult?"

"I don't know that there *is* anything *particular.*"

A long silence.

Anderson said, "I'm going to start timing these silences, Rivers."

"It's already been done. Some of the younger ones had a sweepstake on it. I'm not supposed to know."

"Blood."

"And you attribute this to the ten amputations a day?"

"No, I was all right then. The . . . er . . . problem started later. I wasn't at Étaples when it happened, I'd been moved forward—the 13th CCS. They brought in this lad. He was a Frenchman, he'd escaped from the German lines. Covered in mud. There wasn't an inch of skin showing anywhere. And you know it's not like ordinary mud, it's five, six inches thick. Bleeding. Frantic with pain. No English." A pause. "I missed it. I treated the minor wounds and missed the major one." He gave a short, hissing laugh. "Not that the minor ones were all that minor. He started to haemorrhage, and . . . there was nothing I could do. I just stood there and watched him bleed to death." His face twisted. "It pumped out of him."

It was a while before either of them stirred. Then Anderson said, "If you're wondering why that one, I don't know. I've seen many worse deaths."

"Have you told your family?"

"No. They know I don't like the idea of going back to medicine, but they don't know why."

"Have you talked to your wife?"

"Now and then. You have to think about the *practicalities*, Rivers. I've devoted all my adult life to medicine. I've no private income to tide me over. And I do have *a wife and a child.*"

"Public health might be a possibility."

"It doesn't have much . . . *dash* about it, does it?"

"Is that a consideration?"

Anderson hesitated. "Not with me."

"Well, we can talk about the practicalities later. You still haven't told me when you said *enough.*"

Anderson smiled. "You make it sound like a decision. I don't know that lying on the floor in a pool of piss counts as a decision." He paused. "The following morning. *On the ward.* I remember them all looking down at me. Awkward situation, really. What do you do when the doctor breaks down?"

At intervals, as Rivers was doing his rounds as orderly officer for the day, he thought about this dream. It was disturbing in many ways. At first he'd been inclined to see the post-mortem apron as expressing no more than a lack of faith in *him,* or, more accurately, in his methods, since obviously any doctor who spends much time so attired is not meeting with uniform success on the wards. This lack of faith he knew to be present. Anderson, in his first interview, had virtually refused treatment, claiming that rest, the endless pursuit of golf balls, was all that he required. He had some knowledge of Freud, though derived mainly from secondary or prejudiced sources, and disliked, or perhaps feared, what he thought he knew. There was no particular reason why Anderson, who was, after all, a surgeon, should be well informed about Freudian therapy, but his misconceptions had resulted in a marked reluctance to reveal his dreams. Yet his dreams could hardly be ignored, if only because they were currently keeping the whole of one floor of the hospital awake. His room-mate, Featherstone, had deteriorated markedly as the result of Anderson's nightly outbursts. Still, that was another problem. As soon as Anderson had revealed that extreme horror of blood, Rivers had begun tentatively to attach another meaning to the post-mortem apron. If Anderson could see no way out of returning to the practice of a profession which must inevitably, even in civilian life, recall the horrors he'd witnessed in France, then perhaps he was desperate enough to have considered suicide? That might account both for the post-mortem apron and for the extreme terror he'd felt on waking. At the moment he didn't know Anderson well enough to be able to say whether suicide was a possibility or not, but it would certainly need to be borne in mind.

✂

"THE GREEN TALK"

M. F. K. Fisher (1909–1992) was an American memoirist and essayist best known for her keen observations on the pleasures of eating.
Her collected volume of earlier works, *The Art of Eating,* was published in 1954. "The Green Talk," a departure from this subject, was
taken from her final book, *Last House: Reflections, Dreams, and
Observations, 1943–1991.*

*T*wo nights ago I worked for a long time,
mostly in my subconscious, I suppose, on finding out about
the Green Talk.

In my dream, the Green Talk was in the same class with
ESP, and the ability to use it varied with people, so that June
Eddy, for instance, could speak the Green Talk more easily
and naturally than could I or Joe Abegg, or other people I was
apparently concerned with that night.

If a person has any capacity for it at all—and most of us
live and die unaware of it—it can be consciously developed,
through exercise directed by someone who has the gift
strongly. Apparently it is best to live very closely with such
a person in order to attain any skill. For instance, married
people often have the Green Talk.

In itself, the Green Talk is the ability to speak without
sound—a kind of transference of speech from one spirit to
another. When people use it well, questions can be asked and
answered without any physical contact: expressions in the

eyes or mouth, touch, or of course sound. What is best, and rarest, is that long and witty conversations can go on, between two or more people who have the gift for Green Talk and who have exercised it deliberately—*practiced,* that is.

I cannot remember from the dream whether it is used in prisons, but I rather think so, if the right people are confined together long enough (as in marriage?!).

In the dream (it has already lost its sharp edges, but the fact that I still think about parts of it makes it worth holding on to), I had enough of a gift for the Green Talk to work on it, and several friends helped me. As I became more at ease with it, through their gently patient help in communicating, I felt an increasing sense of pleasure. It was delightful to be in communication with other minds that attracted mine. Of course, this idea that there are two or three levels of speech that can go on in one person has often been written about—I think of a long play by Eugene O'Neill—but I don't remember ever hearing about the Green Talk. In that old play, which interested me very much when I saw and then read it, the third language existed solely within the person who spoke it. The Green Talk, in contrast, is strictly for communication between two or more people. It is not at all secret, and can be picked up by anyone who knows it—or rather, who is aware that it is being spoken and who can go along . . .

I am sure that at its best, it can be used by two skilled people at long distance, much as letters can be exchanged, or voice by telephone or wireless or satellite. In my dream, my own experiments were limited by my fumbling ignorance of the potential within me, and I had to be in the same room or garden or elevator in order to speak it, even with a person much more in control than I. There was no need for any physical contact, although apparently there had to be sympathy, even love—and of course familiarity.

Once this invisible contact was established, no matter how clumsily, I had an almost exalted feeling of enjoyment, of success, of having grown a little farther past the terrible blind limitations of *matter*.

There is no doubt that this feeling of having opened one more tiny door is attained in true meditation, which of course takes great self-discipline and training. It is an inner triumph, and one that I know only indirectly, except for a few instants of realization that flashed upon me and then past me as if to show what *could* be done. But the Green Talk is not meant for anything but communication. In my dream, there was no fear that it would or could be abused, as the telephone can be. The Green Talk is not an instrument but a way . . . and it interested me, even as my subconscious explored it a little, that I could recognize my own limits of attainment. There was no false modesty about this, any more than there is when I know that my skills as a writer, by now developed about as far as they can be, are infinitely smaller than many people's. In the dream, June, for instance, was so much more at ease with the Green Talk than I could ever be that I felt a warm deep gratitude for her for even bothering to help me stumble along. It was rather like a dialogue between Gandhi and a first-year Methodist minister . . . between Einstein and a high school math teacher. But there was nothing but gentle patience toward me as a learner, and June and several other people helped me slowly to speak the Green Talk. My sister Anne was there for a while; several other people I have known, and many I have never consciously met before, began to communicate easily but in what I knew was a simplified way with me.

Always there was the feeling of joyfulness.

I don't know why this form of inaudible invisible conversation is called the Green Talk, but all the time I was dreaming, I kept reminding myself to hang on to the name, to remember it deliberately in the flash before consciousness, and to repeat it sternly because of its terrible importance. This I did, even while I tried to continue the dream explanation. (This process, often used by deliberate dreamers, is much like trying to prolong and hold on to a sexual orgasm, I think.)

Why "green"? Why "talk," even?

To answer that last question, the communication was clearly in words, phrases, sentences. It was not simply a wordless understanding, the kind often experienced even by dull people—the rush of love or compassion, the fleeting exchange of recognition that often flows between people in buses, on streets, in beds. The Green Talk was *talk,* but it was silent.

It went on, perhaps, in the same way that a skilled pianist will play on a silent keyboard while he travels in a plane or bus, or even will move his fingers in his sleep to the sounds his mind conjures. The Green Talk could be carried on at a large dinner party, in a quiet room where only two or three worked or sat or lay, or in a crowded public place. But it took two people. That is perhaps the crux of it—two or, sometimes in my dream, several. And it need not be an urgent communication. Indeed, it was simply a higher form of inter-talk than most of us are aware of.

And I was the novice, plainly touched by the gift but in a very simple and crude way. I stumbled along, and felt happy and excited. It was one more way to be sensate, *awake,* even if in a dream.

—*St. Helena, California, 1971*

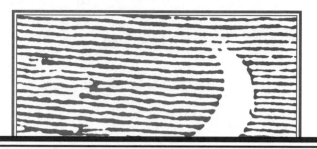

ANXIETY AND
NEUROSIS

FYODOR DOSTOEVSKY

❧

from THE ETERNAL HUSBAND

One of the most influential writers of modern psychological literature, Fyodor Dostoevsky (1821–1881) is author of masterpieces
such as *Crime and Punishment* and *The Brothers Karamazov*. This
Russian novelist wrote *The Eternal Husband* in 1870 while traveling
in Italy and Switzerland. The novel traces the complex relations
between a cuckolded husband, Velchaninov, and his wife's ex-lover,
Pavel Pavlovich, who is by turns sympathetic and murderous.

*T*here is no doubt that Velchaninov did
sleep and that he fell asleep very soon after the candle was put
out; he remembered this clearly afterward. But all the time
he was asleep, up to the very moment that he woke up, he
dreamed that he was not asleep, and that in spite of his
exhaustion he could not fall asleep. At last he began to dream
that he was in a sort of waking delirium, and that he could
not drive away the phantoms that crowded about him,
although he was fully conscious that it was only delirium
and not reality. The phantoms were all familiar figures; his
room seemed to be full of people; and the door into the
passage stood open; people were entering in crowds and
thronging the stairs. At the table, which was set in the middle of the room, a man was sitting—exactly as in a similar
dream he had had a month before. Just as in that dream, this
man sat with his elbows on the table and would not speak;
but this time he was wearing a round hat with crape on it.

"What! Could it have been Pavel Pavlovich that time too?" Velchaninov thought, but, glancing at the face of the silent man, he convinced himself that it was someone quite different. "Why then has he got crape on?" Velchaninov wondered. The noise, the talking, and the shouting of the people crowding round the table was awful. These people seemed to be even more angry at Velchaninov than in the previous dream; they shook their fists at him, and shouted something to him, with all their might, but what it was exactly he could not make out. "But it's delirium, of course, I know it's delirium!" he thought; "I know that I couldn't get to sleep, and that I've got up now because I was too wretched lying down. . . ." But the shouts, the people, their gestures were so lifelike, so real, that sometimes he was seized by doubt: "Can this be really delirium? Good heavens, what do these people want of me? But if this is not delirium, how is it possible that the clamor should not have yet waked Pavel Pavlovich? There he is asleep on the sofa!" At last something suddenly happened again, just as in that other dream; all the people made a rush for the stairs and they were closely packed in the doorway, for there was another crowd forcing its way into the room. These people were bringing something in with them, something big and heavy; you could hear how heavily the steps of those carrying it sounded on the stairs and how hurriedly their panting voices called to one another. All the people in the room shouted, "They're bringing it, they're bringing it," all eyes started flashing and were fixed on Velchaninov; all the people pointed toward the stairs, menacing and triumphant. Now, no longer doubting that this was reality and not delirium, he stood on tiptoe so as to peep over the people's heads and find out as soon as possible what they were carrying up the stairs. His heart was beating, beating,

beating, and suddenly, just as in that earlier dream, the doorbell rang violently three times. And again the sound was so distinct, so real, so unmistakable that it could not be a dream. He screamed and woke up.

JOHN CHEEVER

✣

from THE JOURNALS OF JOHN CHEEVER

An acclaimed American short-story writer and novelist, John Cheever (1912–1982) focused much of his attention on the affluent suburbs of New York. His stories, many of which were first published in *The New Yorker* magazine, have been collected in books such as *The Housebreaker of Shady Hill* and *The World of Apples*. Many of his best-known works were later assembled chronologically in the award-winning *The Stories of John Cheever*. His intensely personal journals were published posthumously in 1990. His dream about Updike reminds readers of the similarities in their writing. Although Cheever was the senior of the two by at least twenty years, both writers have worked a similar fictional territory: the East Coast middle-class suburbs. Their styles are different—Cheever often employed a sharper edge—and yet both often serve to expose similar forms of tension and frustration lurking under this idyllic setting. Beyond the similarities found in their writing one can also gather from this dream that Cheever had probably been paying careful attention to the progress of their careers.

I dream that I am walking with Updike. The landscape seems out of my childhood. A familiar dog barks at us. I see friends and neighbors in their lighted windows. Updike juggles a tennis ball that is both my living and my dying. When he drops the ball I cannot move until it is recovered, and yet I feel, painfully, that he is going to murder me with the ball. He seems murderous and self-possessed. I must try to escape. There is a museum with a turnstile, a marble staircase, and statuary. In the end I do escape.

❧

Joan Didion is an American novelist and essayist noted for her minute depiction of the nihilistic spirit of contemporary culture; she is probably best known for her books focusing on life in 1960s California. These include two collections of essays, *Slouching Toward Bethlehem* and *The White Album,* and her novel *Play It As It Lays.* In this profoundly disturbing novel, Didion creates one of her quintessential heroines, Maria Wyeth, an emotional drifter who, like many of the author's women characters, has almost become anesthetized to the painful and melodramatic events of her life.

$\mathcal{A}$ few days later the dreams began. She was in touch with a member of a shadowy Syndicate. Sometimes the contact was Freddy Chaikin, sometimes an F.B.I. man she had met once in New York and not thought of since. Certain phrases remained constant. Always he explained that he was "part of that operation." Always he wanted to discuss "a business proposition." Always he mentioned a plan to use the house in Beverly Hills for "purposes which would in no way concern" her. She need only supply certain information: the condition of the plumbing, the precise width of the pipes, the location and size of all the clean-outs. Workmen appeared, rooms were prepared. The man in the white duck pants materialized and then the doctor, in his rubber apron. At that point she would fight for consciousness but she was never able to wake herself before the dream revealed its inexorable intention, before the plumbing stopped up, before they all fled and left her there, gray water bubbling up in every sink. Of course she could not call a plumber, because she had known all along what would be found in the pipes, what hacked pieces of human flesh.

GRAHAM GREENE

✖

"ANIMALS WHO TALK"

An English novelist, short-story writer, and journalist, Graham
Greene (1904–1991) is best known for his international novels of
intrigue and psychological suspense, such as *The Ministry of Fear,*
Our Man in Havana, and *The Human Factor.* His posthumously
published *A World of My Own* (1994) contains a selection of dream
diaries he had kept for more than twenty-five years.

*I*t is one of the charms in this World of My
Own that animals talk as intelligibly as human beings. For
example, on the evening of October 18, 1964, I was caressing
a tabby kitten who boasted to me in a small clear voice that
she had killed four birds that day. I rebuked her with pre-
tended anger since I am not very fond of birds. She replied
with a certain pathos, 'But you know, I got forty-two francs
for them.'

I was worried and a little frightened by a beastly little yapping
dog who resented me coming into the house. When I turned
my back on him I could hear him making dashes at my heels.
I shook my finger at him and scolded him and he collapsed
on his side and whimpered out, 'Are you going to punish me?'
I replied, 'I damned well am.' He made a little pool of spittle
in his fear.

In a hut by the sea where I was living I received a visit from a
remarkably intelligent dog. I had met him once before, with

❦

his owner. He had close, curly black hair. He opened the door himself and came and laid his head upon my knee. He asked wistfully, 'Am I faster than Diamond?' Diamond was a cat. I said, 'Yes.'

'Am I faster than. . . .' He mentioned an old spaniel.

'Yes,' I said, 'but remember he's very old.'

Later I had to reprove him for putting his paw on the table laid for two and stretching it towards the sugar basin. I tapped his paw gently and he left the room, opening the door himself and closing it behind him.

In Milan with my friend Yvonne and her setter dog, Sandy. Yvonne went into the cathedral and, when I looked around for Sandy, a bystander told me he had followed her in. But this was not true—it was a different dog. Sandy was lost, and we were about to leave Milan. I went round all the side streets, calling his name with increasing anxiety. At last someone said, 'Here he is,' and a setter bounded towards me with enthusiasm. Only when I had brought him back to the hotel did I realize he was of the wrong colour. So back I went calling 'Sandy!' and to my relief he came. He said to me, 'If only I had carried a handbag with a little money for a taxi. I was lost, and I didn't even know the name of the hotel.'

❦

from ALL MY ROAD BEFORE ME: THE
DIARY OF C. S. LEWIS 1922–1927

C. S. Lewis (1898–1963) was an English novelist, literary scholar,
and essayist on Christian theology and moral issues. His science fiction and children's books, such as the classic *The Chronicles of
Narnia,* were often Christian allegories of good and evil. His early
diaries were for the most part a day-to-day account of his life with
a woman twenty-six years his senior, Mrs. Moore—the mother of a
roommate of his who was killed in the war. She is referred to in his
entries as "D." Throughout these diaries Lewis recorded several of
his dreams. Mrs. Moore and her daughter, Maureen, were present in
many of these.

1923

*W*ednesday *12 September:* I had a most
horrible dream. By a certain poetic justice it turned on the
idea which Jenkin and I were going to use in our shocker play:
namely that of a scientist discovering how to keep consciousness and some motor nerves alive in a corpse, at the
same time arresting decay, so that you really had an immortal dead man. I dreamed that the horrible thing was sent
to us—in a coffin of course—to take care of.

D and Maureen both came into the dream and it was
perfectly ordinary and as vivid as life. Finally the thing
escaped and I fancy ran amuck. It pursued me into a lift in
the Tube in London. I got away all right but the liftman had

❈

seen it and was terribly frightened and, when I saw how he was behaving, I said to myself, "There's going to be an accident in this lift." Just at that moment I noticed the window by my bed and found myself awake.

I had a moment of intense relief but found myself hopelessly rattled and as nervous as a child. I found I had no matches. Groped my way to those on the landing, lit my candle, went downstairs and returned with a pipe and a book. My head was very bad. I got restored to sanity pretty soon and slept, tho' with several breaks before morning. I thought at first that this was a good example of the falsity of the rule given by L.P. Jacks that authors never dream about their own inventions: but on second thoughts I am not sure that the idea of the play did not originate in another dream I had some years ago—unless the whole thing comes from Edgar Allan Poe . . .

SHOLOM ALEICHEM

✧

"ONE IN A MILLION"

A Russian-born Yiddish humorist who emigrated to the United States after escaping the 1905 pogrom in Russia, Sholom Aleichem (1859–1916) is best known for his tales of Jewish life in Eastern European shtetl (villages). His stories about Tevye the milkman received international acclaim when they were transformed into the play *Fiddler on the Roof.* The story "One in a Million" appears in the 1979 collection *The Best of Sholom Aleichem.*

I could swear it's him from head to toe. His slightly hooked nose, his warm, dark, smiling eyes, that one bucktooth that juts out when he starts to laugh. He's no youngster now. He must be my age. And I'm past forty.

Should I approach him? He seems very well dressed—a white vest over his belly, a heavy gold chain, a splendid tie, and from what I've heard, he's living the good life, "in the chips" as they say, a real wheeler-dealer.

I am afraid to say hello. Will he think I'm after something? You should know, I've always considered myself a little proud. Not vain, mind you, just proud.

A proud man scorns the world. Well, it's not that he scorns the world but that the world scorns him—especially if he happens to be poor. There's nothing wrong with poverty—it's no sin, so they say. And knock on wood, I'm no millionaire—far from it. Let's understand each other, I belong to that rich class of the well-disguised poor who cloak their poverty at home behind a mirror and a grand piano and in public

❧

with a showy coat and a new felt hat. But when you really come down to it, they don't even have a crumb to eat or a penny in their pockets.

To be frank, I'm not in the best of straits. Things could be better. I've tried my hand time and again at every kind of hard work and run after enough bad tips—but nothing helps. It's reached such a point I can't stand myself—and neither can others.

Maybe he doesn't give a hoot about me, couldn't care less. The few people who do notice me think, "Watch out, here comes trouble. He wants to wheedle a loan out of me. I won't give him anything." Over my dead body would I ask him for one red cent.

"And how are you?" he asks and looks me straight in the eye.

"How am I?" I say and stare right back.

"How are things going? Pretty well?"

"Not bad."

"Good to hear, thank God," he says and shakes my hand.

"Some people have all the luck," I say to myself and shake his hand.

And so we go our separate ways.

But the person whose story I'm telling didn't look at me like that when we met on the boulevard in Odessa. His look was entirely different. I could read straight into his warm, dark, smiling eyes.

And with those smiling eyes he draws me to him and I feel myself at ease. From afar he stretches out his hand to me. He opens his mouth to laugh and his bucktooth protrudes. "Is it?"

"Could it be?"

We tightly grip each other's hand. I must confess that ever since things have not gone well for me, I can't stand rich people. I can't put up with their healthy, happy, fat faces; I can't bear a face that looks content with itself and the world. But this charmer bends over to me somehow so warmly that we embrace each other.

I don't know how to address him. If I am too familiar, am I taking advantage of our past closeness and reminding him of how time flies? But how can I be formal with him? Didn't we pore over the same texts together for so many years in the same schoolroom?

This very thought must have run through his mind too, for as we start talking, we both use language in such a way that during the entire time we rack our brains to avoid being either too intimate or too formal.

He: I keep looking and looking, maybe it's him, maybe not? How goes it?

I: And I kept thinking the whole time, can it really be him? It looks like him. Maybe it's not? Where is he from?

He: From where? I'm already a native. I've lived in Odessa for who knows how long.

I: And I arrived not too long ago . . . to look for a business.

He: A business? Looking for a business? For me it's just the other way around. I have too much business. If only I had as many good employees! It's bad without good help. And what it costs me each year! ["A braggart," I think to myself.] I don't have any luck with them. How many times have I thought to myself: if I had even one reliable man whom I could trust, it would add ten years to my life. What did I say? Ten? Twenty years for sure! I've already tried to keep all kinds of help—cheap help, expensive help, even very high-priced help—they're all the same, there's not a loyal one among them. I once had so many friends. When one of them came to me seeking help, I would shower him with money from head to foot. ["What a liar!" goes through my mind.] And

✄

as if for spite, I never meet anyone from the old days. I can really say that this is the first time I've had such a meeting since I settled here. It seems to me we once were really close friends, right?

I: Friends? Anything passes for friendship today! We studied together, we boarded together at a rabbi's, we slept on the same bed together.

He: I can even remember at which rabbi's, at Reb Zorah's on top of the Russian stove throughout the whole winter.

I: And summer in the open air on the ground.

He: Like pigs in the muck, with all the frogs.

I: And Tevye the neighbor standing by his broken window screaming at whoever had thrown stones and scaring the entire household half to death.

He: And at Pironditshke's, who swiped the apples right out of the basket with a spiked pole?

I: And the watermelons? Lifted straight off old Gedaliah's wagon at Succos!

And so on.

It isn't easy to stop talking about the good old days. Our memories flow like water from a tap. But he doesn't get down to brass tacks until we come bit by bit to the present and we tell each other about the good and bad in our lives, the happy and the sad.

Things are going well for one of us, very well. With the other, things are going poorly, really badly. One is rich, a millionaire; the other barely ekes out a living. One spares no expense for his children's upbringing: his oldest daughter is happily married off; the sons are all in the finest schools. The other eats his heart out about his children: his eldest daughter wants to give private lessons and has no students, and his son can't get into the first-rate school. You need "pull" and it costs a lot. One has his own house in Odessa with a garden, all sorts of antiques—in short, a paradise. The other has been wandering a good number of years from one hole to the next. Not too long ago they "took inventory of him" from head to foot, sold his bedding, and threw him out on the street. Steeling himself—"what will be, will be"—he moved to another city! They say it's an answer: "Move away and your luck will change!"

With no one else have I ever opened my heart so fully as now with my friend. And no one else listens with such interest to the bitter end. I feel a load off my chest, a weight off my mind. And I notice how his warm, dark, smiling eyes are moist, and he says to me: "That's enough. Things will be better, I swear it. 'Move away and your luck will change.' I know from my own experience; once things did not turn out well for me either. From now on we will be together again."

"What do you mean," I ask, "by 'together'?"

"What 'by together' means?" he says in a singsong, and his warm, dark eyes are laughing. "'By together' means, when someone has a business and needs help desperately and looks for someone—an honest man, a loyal man, no matter what he costs he's worth twice as much—and with God's help he meets a friend of his whom he hasn't seen for such a long time and learns that unfortunately time hasn't treated his friend well and he's looking for a business, it means simply, they need each other. And what could be better than that today?"

And in order to make this bit of luck seem more real, he draws out his wallet, opens it, and wants to show me a telegram. But my eyes don't fix of the telegram but fall on the wad of bills in his wallet—a nice thick wad of crisp bills in hundreds and five hundreds. And my eyes apparently are wide open, and his eyes meet mine and he guesses why I'm staring and says again in the same singsong: "The business,

✖

thank God, can bear it all. And when a new person enters the firm, he needs I'm sure a little extra cash. And there's enough money so why should he not take as much as he needs? What is there to be ashamed of? We all understand what it means to move to a new place with children. I know from experience. I was once in no better shape. I dreamt about greenbacks, too."

And my friend sits down on a bench with me and tells his whole life's story, full of extraordinary events, like tales from the *Thousand and One Nights.* My own life—even with my present troubles—is a bowl of cherries compared to his. I look at him and wonder, "What one man can endure!" And if God could help him after so many troubles, perhaps there's hope for me, too.

And my friend pulls out his wallet again and puts it right under my nose. "Why should one feel embarrassed?" he says to me. "One should take as much as one needs to tide one over."

I ask myself if this isn't a dream and look into the open wallet, and the hundred and five-hundred bills smile at me as do my friend's eyes, and I extend my hand and say: "Two will be enough."

I don't know what I should say: two one hundreds or two five hundreds? And to make it easier for me, he says, "Two thousand, I think, won't go very far."

And he counts out six five-hundred bills and says, "Is three thousand enough on the first go-round?"

"Ah . . ." I couldn't say one word more and fold the wad of bills and stuff them into my breast pocket and feel a strange warmth from them, a soothing feeling.

"And so I won't be embarrassed," he adds, "And I should really like to take a look at my old friend's children, may they be well!"

But I don't answer him immediately. My thoughts are elsewhere—there in the breast pocket with a wad of five hundreds which warm and caress me and will not leave me alone. And my thoughts lead to my wife and children. I imagine the happy scene when they suddenly will see so much money and hear of this good luck.

"Well," I say, "we can go straight to my place. I live a few doors away. The children must be home. Shall we go?"

"Why not?" he says, and I can see in his eyes that he knows my thoughts are on the money in my breast pocket because I automatically pat it and sigh with pleasure. And he, that dog, completely understands, and drags the conversation back to those old, foolish, happy days of our childhood and recalls long-forgotten moments as we make our way to my place.

And then I start thinking about my place, my furniture . . . and I am embarrassed for my rich friend and begin to make excuses: "A new apartment . . . recently moved in . . . summertime . . . not yet settled in."

He understands at once what I mean, and before I can go on he says: "Oh, my . . . the usual . . . it's the same thing all over! No better at my place. Come summer and everything's upside down."

And at the same moment I remember the money flat against my chest and it warms and heats and ignites my thoughts. What shall I do first? . . . And quickly I add up in my mind: rent, the butcher bill, the child's tuition, my wife's shoes, my daughter's hat, a coat for myself, some furniture . . . today's debts, yesterday's debts, debts, debts!

Before I know it, the door is opened and one of my children comes toward me looking very sad. My poor children, I'm afraid, know we can't make ends meet. They know what it is to be poor. Not to be able to buy milk or meat at the market. In the morning the rent collector is coming, along with the woman who supplies us with tea, and the wood man, a brazen youth with a short beard who jeers from far off: "For the wood, you could have paid three times over already."

"Where's mother?" I ask.

"In the kitchen," the child answers.

"We have no maid now. The maid just went off yesterday," I explain to my rich friend and almost die from shame. And I wonder how my wife will enter, Heaven forbid with greasy hands and God-knows-what clothes.

"It's the same at my place," he says. "They come and go; we have a new maid every week."

I don't know what to do. Shall I let my friend remain seated while I go myself into the kitchen and announce the good news to my wife? That miracles do happen? Or would it be better to remain here with my friend in the parlor?

I say "in the parlor" as if there really were a parlor. A large room, yes, but empty, bare—that is, a few tables, a rug, an old piano, a mirror, plus a lamp (a real ugly one), and a bed smack in the middle of the parlor! And still not made so late in the day! I would give a crisp one-hundred right away just to have someone remove the bed from there. My face turns red.

My friend guesses why I'm acting so strangely and calls out: "A nice apartment—airy, roomy, and not a bad idea to have someone sleep in the parlor. At my place, too, the children sleep in the parlor during the summertime."

"Here comes my only son," and I introduce him to my son who decides, just then, to take off his boots and walk around barefoot. My friend seeing that this little scene bothers me, thinks up a white lie: "In summertime—all my children go barefoot, too."

And then my daughter enters, the second oldest. I present her to my old friend. She turns red as a beet, not because

✢

she is shy, but because she is so plainly, even poorly dressed. And the proof is in the shoes—everyday shoes but with patches, without heels, bent out of shape and torn.

And just for spite she sits down in such a way that he sees the shoes, and she notices where he's looking, and I notice how they both are staring at her shoes and I'm ready to die. Give me a hole in the ground, I would jump in alive.

"A lovely child," he whispers in my ear, "pretty as a picture."

I want to say something in reply when my eldest daughter, a real beauty, enters. At least she is wearing a decent pair of shoes, but she has put on a jacket made of thin muslin worn out at the elbows. She's not aware that there is a hole at the elbow and she sinks into her chair a little too deeply so that the elbow juts out straight at him. He looks at the elbow, and I look at him. I wink at her. She doesn't understand, becomes red as a beet, gets up and turns her back to go. Don't look, what a mess: her whole jacket is in shreds.

"One's more beautiful than the other," whispers my friend. "With such fine-looking children one must begin saving for the dowry immediately."

"The hell with this guy and his modern stove, his fancy house and courtyard, and all courtyards. They can all go to hell with Odessa itself for all I care."

By now you must have guessed: it's my grumbling wife who enters from the kitchen, bathed in sweat and burning up, the poor thing, without a maid. She must cook the food all by herself—something she has never been used to. The coal stove is smoking, the butcher will no longer give meat on credit, the milkmaid keeps demanding her money and won't leave the kitchen; in the market everything's overpriced; and

❧

the children carry on—they want new potatoes for lunch with sweet butter, no less!

I want to stop her, to call her away, first to announce the good news and second to have her change her clothes. But my friend doesn't let me, he holds me back and says: "I'd prefer introducing myself."

And he goes up to her, presents himself, and a dialogue ensues:

He: I knew your husband, madam, way before you.

She: A rare piece of luck!

He: We've been friends from childhood on.

She: Tell me who your friends are and I'll tell you who you are.

He: We studied together, ate together, slept together, and even stole apples from a basket together.

She: That speaks well for both of you.

He: Not only apples alone, but watermelons, too.

She: That's enough. I already know who you are.

My wife pronounces the last few words with so much venom that my friend can't say a word. I wink to her, I give her a high sign with my eyes to stop her sharp needling talk. But she's wound up and answers me: "What are you winking for? I know this type, this friend of yours."

"Madam!" says my friend with the voice of a man who feels himself somewhat insulted. "Madam, from what I see, you don't hold your husband in high esteem. May I remind you that I know him better than you."

"May I remind you," answers my wife in the same words, "that no one asked your opinion. He can stand on his own two feet and doesn't need your help."

I see my friend's face change. His cheeks turn flaming red. The warm, dark, smiling eyes have stopped sparkling and he is sweating as if his life were at stake. What shall I do? I'm finished. I may as well end it all. My surprise has turned sour, ruined. I've forgotten about the money in my breast pocket, I've forgotten about everything. Only one thing remains in my head: How can I take my wife aside? How do I let her know what he has done for us? I plead with my eyes: "Keep quiet! Stop talking!" And just for spite, she speaks up.

"I know all about his good friends and old schoolmates!" she says. "Nothing good will come of it. They're either good-for-nothing bums, or big shots dropping by with a story. Just last week a friend of his showed up from his home town, such a close friend, and from so far away—may he go to hell—and sold my husband such a bill of goods that our heads swirled: he's a real millionaire, a big philanthropist, a soft touch, only one of his kind in the world. And when it came time for my husband to ask for . . . What are you getting all embarrassed for? He's a good friend of yours, isn't he, with whom you once stole apples. And when it came time for my husband to tell him that . . ."

I cannot stand it anymore. I'm losing my temper. I can barely see straight. I must stop this talk at once. And I shout to my wife with a voice that's not mine: "That's eeeeee—nough!!!!!!!"

"What's the matter? Why are you screaming? Wake up!" blurts my wife, frightened to death, and shakes me out of sleep.

I sit up, rub my eyes, and look around. "Where can he be?"

"Who? Whom are you looking for?"

"My blood brother, that friend of mine."

"What blood brother? What friend? You were dreaming. Spit three times to ward off the evil eye! You went to bed late.

How many times have I told you that you should stop writing late at night?"

I reach for my pocket and feel for the money. God, it was just there, just as I left it. A wad of crisp five-hundreds! I can still hear the crackle and feel the fresh bills in my hand.

And I remember that tomorrow at ten in the morning the tax collector is coming to draw up a list and auction off my chairs, and the landlord is throwing me out of the apartment, and the butcher wants his money and the milkmaid wants hers, and the woodcutter won't stop either—he comes by all the time and repeats, "Can't pay yet?" . . . And my son has an announcement: he's ready for his exams. Good luck to you, son, you should live to give better news. . . .

I'm bathing in sweat and trembling with chills.

MARGARET ATWOOD

❧

from LADY ORACLE

A Canadian novelist, poet, and critic recognized for bringing a
sardonic level of humor to much of her fiction, Margaret Atwood
exposes the underside of everyday life. In *Lady Oracle,* one of her
wittiest novels, the central character's musings about her husband,
her mother, and herself give the narrative a sharp, ironic edge. The
dream sequence clearly reveals the character's relationship with
her mother.

One of the bad dreams I used to have
about my mother was this. I would be walking across the
bridge and she would be standing in the sunlight on the other
side of it, talking to someone else, a man whose face I couldn't
see. When I was halfway across, the bridge would collapse, as
I'd always feared it would. Its rotten planks buckled and split,
it tilted over sideways and began to topple slowly into the
ravine. I would try to run but it would be too late, I would
throw myself down and grab onto the far edge as it rose up,
trying to slide me off. I called out to my mother, who could
still have saved me, she could have run across quickly and
reached out her hand, she could have pulled me back with her
to firm ground— But she didn't do this, she went on with her
conversation, she didn't notice that anything unusual was
happening. She didn't even hear me.

In the other dream I would be sitting in a corner of my
mother's bedroom, watching her put on her makeup. I did this
often as a small child: it was considered a treat, a privilege, by

❧

both my mother and myself, and refusing to let me watch was one of my mother's ways of punishing me. She knew I was fascinated by her collection of cosmetics and imple ments: lipsticks, rouges, perfume in dainty bottles which I longed to have, bright red nail polish (sometimes, as an exceptional bribe, I was allowed to have some brushed on my toes, but never on my fingers: "You're not old enough," she'd say), little tweezers, nail files and emery boards. I was for bidden to touch any of these things. Of course I did, when she was out, but they were arranged in such rigid rows both on the dressertop and in the drawers that I had to be very care ful to put them back exactly where I'd found them. My mother had a hawk's eye for anything out of place. I later extended this habit of snooping through her drawers and cupboards until I knew everything that each of them con tained; finally I would do it not to satisfy my curiosity— I already knew everything—but for the sense of danger. I only got caught twice, early on: once when I ate a lipstick (even then, at the age of four, I was wise enough to replace the cover on the tube and the tube in the drawer, and to wash my mouth carefully; how did she know it was me?), and once when I couldn't resist covering my entire face with blue eye shadow, to see how I would look blue. That got me exiled for weeks. I almost gave the whole game away the day I found a curious object, like a rubber clamshell, packed away neatly in a box. I was dying to ask her what it was, but I didn't dare.

"Sit there quietly, Joan, and watch Mother put on her face," she'd say on the good days. Then she would tuck a towel around her neck and go to work. Some of the things she did seemed to be painful; for instance, she would cover the space between her eyebrows with what looked like brown glue, which she heated in a little pot, then tear it off, leaving a red patch; and sometimes she'd smear herself with pink mud which would harden and crack. She often frowned at herself, shaking her head as if she was dissatisfied; and occasionally she'd talk to herself as if she'd forgotten I was there. Instead of making her happier, these sessions appeared to make her sadder, as if she saw behind or within the mirror some fleeting image she was unable to capture or duplicate; and when she was finished she was always a little cross.

I would stare at the proceedings, fascinated and mute. I thought my mother was very beautiful, even more beautiful when she was colored in. And this was what I did in the dream: I sat and stared. Although her vanity tables became more grandiose as my father got richer, my mother always had a triple mirror, so she could see both sides as well as the front of her head. In the dream, as I watched, I suddenly realized that instead of three reflections she had three actual heads, which rose from her toweled shoulders on three separate necks. This didn't frighten me, as it seemed merely a confirmation of something I'd always known; but outside the door there was a man, a man who was about to open the door and come in. If he saw, if he found out the truth about my mother, something terrible would happen, not only to my mother but to me. I wanted to jump up, run to the door, and stop him, but I couldn't move and the door would swing inward. . . .

As I grew older, this dream changed. Instead of wanting to stop the mysterious man, I would sit there wishing for him to enter. I wanted him to find out her secret, the secret that I alone knew: my mother was a monster.

FRANZ   KAFKA

✄

from THE   DIARIES   OF   FRANZ   KAFKA
1914–1923

Born and raised in the Jewish enclave of Prague, Franz Kafka
(1883–1924) is best known for his existential fiction, which includes
Metamorphosis, The Trial, and *The Castle.* Many of Kafka's most
famous works, including his diaries, were edited and published
posthumously by his friend Max Brod. Kafka recorded his dreams
on a frequent basis. Although they often reveal the brooding elements of a persecution complex, these writings don't usually offer
an ultimate recognition of the feelings that undermine such an
obsession. In this entry, written in 1921, Kafka exposes a complex
side of his obsessive nature.

A short dream, during an agitated, short
sleep, in agitation clung to it with a feeling of boundless happiness. A dream with many ramifications, full of a thousand
connections that became clear in a flash; but hardly more
than the basic mood remains: My brother had committed a
crime, a murder, I think, I and other people were involved in
the crime; punishment, solution and salvation approached
from afar, loomed up powerfully, many signs indicated their
ineluctable approach; my sister, I think, kept calling out
these signs as they appeared and I kept greeting them with
insane exclamations, my insanity increased as they drew
nearer. I thought I should never be able to forget my frag-
mentary exclamations, brief sentences merely, because of
their succinctness, and now don't clearly remember a single

❡ 157 ❡

one. I could only have uttered brief exclamations because of the great effort it cost me to speak—I had to puff out my cheeks and at the same time contort my mouth as if I had a toothache before I could bring a word out. My feeling of happiness lay in the fact that I welcomed so freely, with such conviction and such joy, the punishment that came, a sight that must have moved the gods, and I felt the gods' emotion almost to the point of tears.

DEATH AND ESCAPE

✖

from "PALE HORSE, PALE RIDER"

Although this American author's one long novel, *Ship of Fools,* written late in her career, became an immediate best-seller, Katherine Anne Porter (1890–1980) is best known as a writer of short stories. Porter's collections include *Flowering Judas* and *The Leaning Tower.* Another, *Collected Stories,* received both a Pulitzer Prize and National Book Award.

*I*n sleep she knew she was in her bed, but not the bed she had lain down in a few hours since, and the room was not the same but it was a room she had known somewhere. Her heart was a stone lying upon her breast outside of her; her pulses lagged and paused, and she knew that something strange was going to happen, even as the early morning winds were cool through the lattice, the streaks of light were dark blue and the whole house was snoring in its sleep.

Now I must get up and go while they are all quiet. Where are my things? Things have a will of their own in this place and hide where they like. Daylight will strike a sudden blow on the roof startling them all up to their feet; faces will beam asking, Where are you going, What are you doing, What are you thinking, How do you feel, Why do you say such things, What do you mean? No more sleep. Where are my boots and what horse shall I ride? Fiddler or Graylie or Miss Lucy with the long nose and the wicked eye? How I have loved this house in the morning before we are all awake and tangled

❧

together like badly cast fishing lines. Too many people have been born here, and have wept too much here, and have laughed too much, and have been too angry and outrageous with each other here. Too many have died in this bed already, there are far too many ancestral bones propped up on the mantelpieces, there have been too damned many anti-macassars in this house, she said loudly, and oh, what accumulation of storied dust never allowed to settle in peace for one moment.

And the stranger? Where is that lank greenish stranger I remember hanging about the place, welcomed by my grandfather, my great-aunt, my five times removed cousin, my decrepit hound and my silver kitten? Why did they take to him, I wonder? And where are they now? Yet I saw him pass the window in the evening. What else besides them did I have in the world? Nothing. Nothing is mine, I have only nothing but it is enough, it is beautiful and it is all mine. Do I even walk about in my own skin or is it something I have borrowed to spare my modesty? Now what horse shall I borrow for this journey I do not mean to take, Graylie or Miss Lucy or Fiddler who can jump ditches in the dark and knows how to get the bit between his teeth? Early morning is best for me because trees are trees in one stroke, stones are stones set in shades known to be grass, there are no false shapes or surmises, the road is still asleep with the crust of dew unbroken. I'll take Graylie because he is not afraid of bridges.

Come now, Graylie, she said, taking his bridle, we must outrun Death and the Devil. You are no good for it, she told the other horses standing saddled before the stable gate, among them the horse of the stranger, gray also, with tarnished nose and ears. The stranger swung into his saddle beside her, leaned far towards her and regarded her without meaning, the blank still stare of mindless malice that makes no threats and can bide its time. She drew Graylie around sharply, urged him to run. He leaped the low rose hedge and the narrow ditch beyond, and the dust of the lane flew heavily under his beating hoofs. The stranger rode beside her, easily, lightly, his reins loose in his half-closed hand, straight and elegant in dark shabby garments that flapped upon his bones; his pale face smiled in an evil trance, he did not glance at her. Ah, I have seen this fellow before, I know this man if I could place him. He is no stranger to me.

She pulled Graylie up, rose in her stirrups and shouted, I'm not going with you this time—ride on! Without pausing or turning his head the stranger rode on. Graylie's ribs heaved under her, her own ribs rose and fell, Oh, why am I so tired, I must wake up. "But let me get a fine yawn first," she said, opening her eyes and stretching, "a slap of cold water in my face, for I've been talking in my sleep again, I heard myself but what was I saying?"

Slowly, unwillingly, Miranda drew herself up inch by inch out of the pit of sleep, waited in a daze for life to begin again. A single word struck in her mind, a gong of warning, reminding her for the day long what she forgot happily in sleep, and only in sleep. The war, said the gong, and she shook her head.

VIRGINIA WOOLF

❈

DIARY ENTRY

While Woolf's reputation was established by the critical success of
novels such as *Mrs. Dalloway, Jacob's Room,* and *To the Lighthouse,*
she was also a prolific journal writer. With the publication of her
eleven diaries in the 1970s, critical interest to her work was renewed.
The entry here was written in 1929, shortly after the publication of
her feminist classic *A Room of One's Own.* Although this book
was off to a successful start, she at the same time was struggling with
her novel *The Waves.* In her dream she seems to be obsessing about
both works.

52 Tavistock Square WC1
Saturday 2 November 1929

I dreamt last night that I had a disease of
the heart that would kill me in six months. Leonard, after
some persuasion, told me. My instincts were all such as
I should have, in order, and some very strong: quite volun-
tary, as they are in dreams, and have thus an authenticity
which makes an immense and pervading impression. First,
relief—well I've done with life anyhow (I was lying in bed);
then horror; then desire to live; then fear of insanity; then (no
this came earlier) regret about my writing, and leaving this
book unfinished; then a luxurious dwelling upon my friends'
sorrow; then a sense of death and being done with at my age;
then telling Leonard that he must marry again; seeing our life

together; and facing the conviction of going, when other people went on living. Then I woke, coming to the top with all this hanging about me; and found I had sold a great many copies of my book—the odd feeling of these two states of life and death mingling as I ate my breakfast feeling drowsy and heavy.

JAMES HILLMAN

✖

"THE DEATH METAPHOR"

James Hillman, one of the most provocative Jungian thinkers
of our time, became the first director of the Jungian Institute in
Zurich in 1959. He is the author of more than a dozen books, including the best-selling *Soul's Code* and the recently published *Dream
Animals.* "The Death Metaphor" was excerpted from *The Dream and
the Underworld.*

W hen I use the word *death* and bring it
into connection with dreams, I run the risk of being misunderstood grossly, since death to us tends to mean exclusively
gross death—physical, literal death. Our emphasis upon
physical death corresponds with our emphasis upon the
physical body, not the subtle one; on physical life, not psychic
life; on the literal and not the metaphorical. That love and
death could be metaphorical is difficult to understand—after
all something must be real says the ego, the great literalist,
positivist, realist. We easily lose touch with the subtle kinds
of death. For us, pollution and decomposition and cancer
have become physical only. We concentrate our propitiations
against one kind of death only, the kind defined by the ego's
sense of reality. The death we speak of in our culture is a fantasy of the ego, and we take our dreams in this same manner.

Our culture is singular for its ignorance of death. The
great art and celebrations of many other cultures—ancient
Egyptian and Etruscan, the Greek of Eleusis, Tibetan—honor

the underworld. We have no ancestor cult, although we are pathetically nostalgic. We keep no relics, though collect antiques. We rarely see dead human beings, though watch a hundred imitations each week on the television tube. The animals we eat are put away out of sight. We have no myths of the *nekyia,* yet our popular heroes in films and music are shady underworld characters. Dante's underworld was our culture's last, and it was imagined even before the Renaissance had properly begun. Our ethnic roots reach back to great underworld configurations: the Celtic Dagda or Cerunnos, the Germanic Hel, and the Biblical Sheol. All have faded; how pale the fire of the Christian Hell. Where have they gone? Where is death when it is no longer observed? Where do contents of consciousness go when they fade from attention? Into the unconscious, says psychology. The underworld has gone into the unconscious: even become the unconscious. Depth psychology is where today we find the initiatory mystery, the long journey of psychic learning, ancestor worship, the encounter with demons and shadows, the sufferings of Hell.

The person who goes into analysis is therefore not an analysand, a client, a pupil, a trainee, or a partner—but a patient. This word is retained, not because of its historical origins in nineteenth-century medicine, as much as because it bespeaks the actual condition of going into the depths of soul. The *soul* is the patient of *psycho*-therapy, and a person (client, partner, analysand) is immediately constellated as soul the moment he or she becomes a patient. The underworld experience turns us each into patients, as well as giving us a new feeling of patience. "In your patience is your soul," was a religious alchemical maxim, saying that soul is found in the reception of its suffering, in the attendance upon it, the waiting it through. From the soul's viewpoint, there is little difference between *patient* and *therapist*. Both words in their roots refer to an attentive devotion, waiting on and waiting for.

Waiting for what? One answer could be: death. Psychotherapy as waiting attendance upon death, dreamwork as deathwork. But this answer would literalize death and lose its metaphorical sense. The Egyptian Ba never dies; the Christian soul is immortal—which means that physical death as the medically and legally defined cessation of life is not the background of dreamwork. This sort of death is again the literal viewpoint of the ego that can't get out of its own life except by dying, which it takes in that same physical manner as it takes everything else. Death is not the background to dreamwork, but soul is. Soul, if immortal, has more to it than dying, and so dreams cannot be limited to attendance upon death. The psychic perspective is focused not only on death or about dying. Rather, it is a consciousness that stands on its own legs only when we have put our dayworld notions to sleep. *Death* is the most profoundly radical way of expressing this shift in consciousness.

Yet how difficult it is to maintain the underworld perspective; how unnatural! After all, we are in life, and we do look at dreams in "sweet daylight." The price of this sunny viewpoint, however, is that death and the fear of it become the fount of psychology's negative predications: 'evil,' 'shadow,' 'unconscious,' 'psychopathic,' 'regressive,' 'stuck,' 'destructive,' 'cut off,' 'unrelated,' 'cold,' as well as the familiar minus sign pasted onto one side of each complex—do these words and signs not mean "tinged with death," as enemies of life and of love? By declaring a situation or a complex negative, do we not truly mean that it is stopping life, that it is death bound, going to Hell; that now we are engaging hopelessness and a primordial coldness that shuns life, or a darkness that wills the worst, impenetrable to reason's clear sight? The negative signs in psychology seem to me to be really a shorthand for the prejudice of a dayworld's Eros against Thanatos. We can therefore only see negatively, the destructive, pessimistic, suicidal components of the psyche and cannot meet with our understanding the depth to which contents would go in Stygian hatred, or when they prefer separations to unions, or take the downward path of inertia into withdrawal, forgetting, and still reflection.

Depth psychology has been the modern movement within our culture that returns to it a sense of the underworld. Since its inception with Freud, depth psychology has been a "movement," driven by a mission. Some of that mission has been the Resurrection of the Dead, the recall of life of so much forgotten and buried in each of us. It did not go far enough, however. It believed that lifting personal or cultural repression of the instinctual id was its end. It opened the tomb, imagining that a mummified body would rise up; but the id as the underworld is not the instinctual body. It is the chthonic psyche. What is most dead and buried in each of us is the culture's neglect of Death. Hades only now begins to reappear in ominous new concerns with the limits to growth, the energy crisis, ecological pollution, ageing and dying.

Not the dead shall rise, but the Resurrection of Death itself; for depth psychology brings back to us not only the persons of the dream and the memorial psyche of the underworld. It has also brought Death back from its exile in the parapsychology of spiritism, the theology of afterlife, the morality of rewards, and the scientific fantasies of biochemical chance or evolution—back to its main place in the midst of the psychological life of each individual, which opens into depth at every step. Our footfalls echo on its vaults

❧

below. There is an opening downward within each moment, an unconscious reverberation, like the thin thread of the dream that we awaken with in our hands each morning leading back and down into the images of the dark.

JOHN   EDGAR   WIDEMAN

⋈

from " H O S T A G E S "

John Edgar Wideman, an American novelist, short-story writer, and critic, is probably best known for his nonfiction work *Brothers and Keepers,* an account of his relationship with a brother serving a life sentence for murder. His novels include *Philadelphia Fire* and the Homewood trilogy, which includes the award-winning *Sent for You Yesterday.*

She remembers two of her dreams: girls playing in a huge, manicured backyard. They are tickled by the coincidence of their names, the fact each contains *Van*— Vanita, Van Tyne, Vanessa, Vanna, Van de Meer, et cetera. They've just discovered this joke and it delights them, but very quickly the mood shifts. Giggles cease, longer and longer gaps of silence. They become aware of the size of the backyard. Its emptiness. There's really no one else to talk to as the identities of the group shrink to one girl. The silliness of the names is a mocking echo in her mind. The others have *van*ished. Far away, trailing the squeal and thunder of an old-fashioned engine, boxcars wobble along clickedy-click on toy wheels, like ducks bobbing, wise old heads nodding, sucking on pipes, puffing silent rings of smoke. She is weary and lonely. The jabbering of her friends, the syllable *Van* they shared are part of the weight this yard has accumulated. Its history bears down on her.

If she doesn't awaken from this next dream she'll be dead. But if she awakens, it will be two in the morning and worse than death. She will blunder around in the darkness, drink water, pop a pill, sit on the toilet. Sleep won't come again for hours. Her heart thumps and sputters. Not enough air. Her lungs ache. A bear scratches at the window. She's alert now. Resigned, she lifts the covers and cool, merciful air infiltrates the clamminess beneath the blankets she steeples with her knees. A slab of icy hip beside her. Someone naked and dead in her bed. She is afraid to move. She knows it's her body lying next to her and the thought of touching it again paralyzes her. She's soaked in her own sweat. Thick as blood or paint. She can't see its color but knows it's dark. The color of her lover, a man whose sweat turns her to a tar baby too, wet and black and sticky. She will die if she moves, if she doesn't. If she opens her eyes, the iridescent clock will say 2:00 A.M.

JULIO CORTÁZAR

✿

"THE NIGHT FACE UP"

An Argentine writer born in Brussels, Belgium, Julio Cortázar (1914–1984) often drew on the metaphysical themes of life, death, time, and the power of the imagination. His short story "Blow-Up," included in *End of the Game and Other Stories,* was the subject of a successful and provocative film adaptation by Michelangelo Antonioni. Other Cortázar works include *A Change of Light and Other Stories* and his internationally acclaimed experimental novel *Hopscotch.*

*H*alfway down the long hotel vestibule, he thought that probably he was going to be late, and hurried on into the street to get out his motorcycle from the corner where the next-door superintendent let him keep it. On the jewelry store at the corner he read that it was ten to nine; he had time to spare. The sun filtered through the tall down-town buildings, and he—because for himself, for just going along thinking, he did not have a name—he swung onto the machine, savoring the idea of the ride. The motor whirred between his legs, and a cool wind whipped his pantslegs.

He let the ministries zip past (the pink, the white), and a series of stores on the main street, their windows flashing. Now he was beginning the most pleasant part of the run, the real ride: a long street bordered with trees, very little traffic, with spacious villas whose gardens rambled all the way down to the sidewalks, which were barely indicated by low hedges. A bit inattentive perhaps, but tooling along on the right side

❧

of the street, he allowed himself to be carried away by the freshness, by the weightless contraction of this hardly begun day. This involuntary relaxation, possibly, kept him from preventing the accident. When he saw that the woman standing on the corner had rushed into the crosswalk while he still had the green light, it was already somewhat too late for a simple solution. He braked hard with foot and hand, wrenching himself to the left; he heard the woman scream, and at the collision his vision went. It was like falling asleep all at once.

He came to abruptly. Four or five young men were getting him out from under the cycle. He felt the taste of salt and blood, one knee hurt, and when they hoisted him up he yelped, he couldn't bear the pressure on his right arm. Voices which did not seem to belong to the faces hanging above him encouraged him cheerfully with jokes and assurances. His single solace was to hear someone else confirm that the lights indeed had been in his favor. He asked about the woman, trying to keep down the nausea which was edging up into his throat. While they carried him face up to a nearby pharmacy, he learned that the cause of the accident had gotten only a few scrapes on the legs. "Nah, you barely got her at all, but when ya hit, the impact made the machine jump and flop on its side . . ." Opinions, recollections of other smashups, take it easy, work him in shoulders first, there, that's fine, and someone in a dustcoat giving him a swallow of something soothing in the shadowy interior of the small local pharmacy.

Within five minutes the police ambulance arrived, and they lifted him onto a cushioned stretcher. It was a relief for him to be able to lie out flat. Completely lucid, but realizing that he was suffering the effects of a terrible shock, he gave his information to the officer riding in the ambulance with him. The arm almost didn't hurt; blood dripped down from a cut over the eyebrow all over his face. He licked his lips once

✣

or twice to drink it. He felt pretty good, it had been an accident, tough luck; stay quiet a few weeks, nothing worse. The
guard said that the motorcycle didn't seem badly racked up.
"Why should it," he replied. "It all landed on top of me." They
both laughed, and when they got to the hospital, the guard
shook his hand and wished him luck. Now the nausea was
coming back little by little; meanwhile they were pushing him
on a wheeled stretcher toward a pavilion further back, rolling
along under trees full of birds, he shut his eyes and wished he
were asleep or chloroformed. But they kept him for a good
while in a room with that hospital smell, filling out a form,
getting his clothes off, and dressing him in a stiff, greyish
smock. They moved his arm carefully, it didn't hurt him. The
nurses were constantly making wisecracks, and if it hadn't
been for the stomach contractions he would have felt fine,
almost happy.

They got him over to X-ray, and twenty minutes later,
with the still-damp negative lying on his chest like a black
tombstone, they pushed him into surgery. Someone tall
and thin in white came over and began to look at the X-rays.
A woman's hands were arranging his head, he felt that they
were moving him from one stretcher to another. The man in
white came over to him again, smiling, something gleamed in
his right hand. He patted his cheek and made a sign to someone stationed behind.

It was unusual as a dream because it was full of smells, and
he never dreamt smells. First a marshy smell, there to the left
of the trail the swamps began already, the quaking bogs from
which no one ever returned. But the reek lifted, and instead
there came a dark, fresh composite fragrance, like the night
under which he moved, in flight from the Aztecs. And it was
all so natural, he had to run from the Aztecs who had set out

✺

on their manhunt, and his sole chance was to find a place to hide in the deepest part of the forest, taking care not to lose the narrow trail which only they, the Motecas, knew.

What tormented him the most was the odor, as though, notwithstanding the absolute acceptance of the dream, there was something which resisted that which was not habitual, which until that point had not participated in the game. "It smells of war," he thought, his hand going instinctively to the stone knife which was tucked at an angle into his girdle of woven wool. An unexpected sound made him crouch suddenly stock-still and shaking. To be afraid was nothing strange, there was plenty of fear in his dreams. He waited, covered by the branches of a shrub and the starless night. Far off, probably on the other side of the big lake, they'd be lighting the bivouac fires; that part of the sky had a reddish glare. The sound was not repeated. It had been like a broken limb. Maybe an animal that, like himself, was escaping from the smell of war. He stood erect slowly, sniffing the air. Not a sound could be heard, but the fear was still following, as was the smell, that cloying incense of the war of the blossom. He had to press forward, to stay out of the bogs and get to the heart of the forest. Groping uncertainly through the dark, stooping every other moment to touch the packed earth of the trail, he took a few steps. He would have liked to have broken into a run, but the gurgling fens lapped on either side of him. On the path and in darkness, he took his bearings. Then he caught a horrible blast of that foul smell he was most afraid of, and leaped forward desperately.

"You're going to fall off the bed," said the patient next to him. "Stop bouncing around, old buddy."

He opened his eyes and it was afternoon, the sun already low in the oversized windows of the long ward. While trying to smile at his neighbor, he detached himself almost physically from the final scene of the nightmare. His arm, in a plaster cast, hung suspended from an apparatus with weights and pulleys. He felt thirsty, as though he'd been running for miles, but they didn't want to give him much water, barely enough to moisten his lips and make a mouthful. The fever was winning slowly and he would have been able to sleep again, but he was enjoying the pleasure of keeping awake, eyes half-closed, listening to the other patients' conversation, answering a question from time to time. He saw a little white pushcart come up beside the bed, a blond nurse rubbed the front of his thigh with alcohol and stuck him with a fat needle connected to a tube which ran up to a bottle filled with a milky, opalescent liquid. A young intern arrived with some metal and leather apparatus which he adjusted to fit onto the good arm to check something or other. Night fell, and the fever went along dragging him down softly to a state in which things seemed embossed as through opera glasses, they were real and soft and, at the same time, vaguely distasteful; like sitting in a boring movie and thinking that, well, still, it'd be worse out in the street, and staying.

A cup of a marvelous golden broth came, smelling of leeks, celery and parsley. A small hunk of bread, more precious than a whole banquet, found itself crumbling little by little. His arm hardly hurt him at all, and only in the eyebrow where they'd taken stitches a quick, hot pain sizzled occasionally. When the big windows across the way turned to smudges of dark blue, he thought it would not be difficult for him to sleep. Still on his back so a little uncomfortable, running his tongue out over his hot, too-dry lips, he tasted the broth still, and with a sigh of bliss, he let himself drift off.

First there was confusion, as of one drawing all his sensations, for that moment blunted or muddled, into himself. He realized that he was running in pitch darkness, although, above, the sky criss-crossed with treetops was less black than the rest. "The trail," he thought, "I've gotten off the trail." His feet sank into a bed of leaves and mud, and then he couldn't take a step that the branches of shrubs did not whiplash against his ribs and legs. Out of breath, knowing despite the darkness and silence that he was surrounded, he crouched down to listen. Maybe the trail was very near, with the first daylight he would be able to see it again. Nothing now could help him to find it. The hand that had unconsciously gripped the haft of the dagger climbed like a fen scorpion up to his neck where the protecting amulet hung. Barely moving his lips, he mumbled the supplication of the corn which brings about the beneficent moons, and the prayer to Her Very Highness, to the distributor of all Motecan possessions. At the same time he felt his ankles sinking deeper into the mud, and the waiting in the darkness of the obscure grove of live oak grew intolerable to him. The war of the blossom had started at the beginning of the moon and had been going on for three days and three nights now. If he managed to hide in the depths of the forest, getting off the trail further up past the marsh country, perhaps the warriors wouldn't follow his track. He thought of the many prisoners they'd already taken. But the number didn't count, only the consecrated period. The hunt would continue until the priests gave the sign to return. Everything had its number and its limit, and it was within the sacred period, and he on the other side from the hunters.

He heard the cries and leaped up, knife in hand. As if the sky were aflame on the horizon, he saw torches moving among the branches, very near him. The smell of war was unbearable, and when the first enemy jumped him, leaped at his throat, he felt an almost-pleasure in sinking the stone blade flat to the haft into his chest. The lights were already around him, the happy cries. He managed to cut the air once or twice, then a rope snared him from behind.

"It's the fever," the man in the next bed said. "The same thing happened to me when they operated on my duodenum. Take some water, you'll see, you'll sleep all right."

Laid next to the night from which he came back, the tepid shadow of the ward seemed delicious to him. A violet lamp kept watch high on the far wall like a guardian eye. You could hear coughing, deep breathing, once in a while a conversation in whispers. Everything was pleasant and secure, without the chase, no . . . But he didn't want to go on thinking about the nightmare. There were lots of things to amuse himself with. He began to look at the cast on his arm, and the pulleys that held it so comfortably in the air. They'd left a bottle of mineral water on the night table beside him. He put the neck of the bottle to his mouth and drank it like a precious liqueur. He could now make out the different shapes in the ward, the thirty beds, the closets with glass doors. He guessed that his fever was down, his face felt cool. The cut over the eyebrow barely hurt at all, like a recollection. He saw himself leaving the hotel again, wheeling out the cycle. Who'd have thought that it would end like this? He tried to fix the moment of the accident exactly, and it got him very angry to notice that there was a void there, an emptiness he could not manage to fill. Between the impact and the moment that they picked him up off the pavement, the passing out or what went on, there was nothing he could see. And at the same time he had the feeling that this void, this nothingness, had lasted an eternity. No, not even time, more as if, in this void, he had passed across something, or had run back immense distances. The shock, the brutal dashing against the pavement. Anyway, he had felt an immense relief in coming out of the black pit while the people were lifting him off the ground. With pain in the broken arm, blood from the split eyebrow, contusion on the knee; with all that, a relief in returning to daylight, to the day, and to feel sustained and attended. That was weird. Someday he'd ask the doctor at the office about that. Now sleep began to take over again, to pull him slowly down. The pillow was so soft, and the coolness of the mineral water in his fevered throat. The violet light of the lamp up there was beginning to get dimmer and dimmer.

As he was sleeping on his back, the position in which he came to did not surprise him, but on the other hand the damp smell, the smell of oozing rock, blocked his throat and forced him to understand. Open the eyes and look in all directions, hopeless. He was surrounded by an absolute darkness. Tried to get up and felt ropes pinning his wrists and ankles. He was staked to the ground on a floor of dank, icy stone slabs. The cold bit into his naked back, his legs. Dully, he tried to touch the amulet with his chin and found they had stripped him of it. Now he was lost, no prayer could save him from the final . . . From afar off, as though filtering through the rock of the dungeon, he heard the great kettledrums of the feast. They had carried him to the temple, he was in the underground cells of Teocalli itself, awaiting his turn.

He heard a yell, a hoarse yell that rocked off the walls. Another yell, ending in a moan. It was he who was screaming in the darkness, he was screaming because he was alive, his whole body with that cry fended off what was coming, the inevitable end. He thought of his friends filling up the other dungeons, and of those already walking up the stairs of the sacrifice. He uttered another choked cry, he could barely open his mouth, his jaws were twisted back as if with a rope and a stick, and once in a while they would open slowly with an endless exertion, as if they were made of rubber. The creaking of the wooden latches jolted him like a whip. Rent, writhing, he fought to rid himself of the cords sinking into his flesh. His right arm, the strongest, strained until the pain became unbearable and he had to give up. He watched the double door open, and the smell of the torches reached him before the light did. Barely girdled by the ceremonial loin-cloths, the priests' acolytes moved in his direction, looking at him with contempt. Lights reflected off the sweaty torsos and off the black hair dressed with feathers. The cords went slack, and in their place the grappling of hot hands, hard as bronze; he felt himself lifted, still face up, and jerked along by the four acolytes who carried him down the passageway. The torch-bearers went ahead, indistinctly lighting up the corridor with its dripping walls and a ceiling so low that the acolytes had to duck their heads. Now they were taking him out, taking him out, it was the end. Face up, under a mile of living rock which, for a succession of moments, was lit up by a glimmer of torchlight. When the stars came out up there instead of the roof and the great terraced steps rose before him, on fire with cries and dances, it would be the end. The passage was never going to end, but now it was beginning to end, he would see suddenly the open sky full of stars, but not yet, they trundled him along endlessly in the reddish shadow, hauling him roughly along and he did not want that, but how to stop it if they had torn off the amulet, his real heart, the life-center.

In a single jump he came out into the hospital night, to the high, gentle, bare ceiling, to the soft shadow wrapping him round. He thought he must have cried out, but his neigh-bors were peacefully snoring. The water in the bottle on the night table was somewhat bubbly, a translucent shape against the dark azure shadow of the windows. He panted, looking for some relief for his lungs, oblivion for those images still glued to his eyelids. Each time he shut his eyes he saw them take shape instantly, and he sat up, completely wrung out, but savoring at the same time the surety that now he was awake, that the night nurse would answer if he rang, that soon it would be daybreak, with the good, deep sleep he usually had at that hour, no images, no nothing . . . It was difficult to keep his eyes open, the drowsiness was more powerful than he. He made one last effort, he sketched a gesture toward the bottle of water with his good hand and did not manage to reach it, his fingers closed again on a black emptiness, and the passageway went on endlessly, rock after rock, with momentary ruddy flares, and face up he choked out a dull moan because the roof was about to end, it rose, was opening like a mouth of shadow, and the acolytes straightened up, and from on high a waning moon fell on a face whose eyes wanted not to see it, were closing and opening desperately, trying to pass to the other side, to find again the bare, protecting ceiling of the ward. And every time they opened, it was night and the moon, while they climbed the great terraced steps, his head hanging down backward now, and up at the top were the bonfires, red columns of perfumed smoke, and suddenly he saw the red stone, shiny with the blood dripping off it, and the spinning arcs cut by the feet of the victim whom they pulled off to throw him rolling down the north steps. With a last hope he shut his lids tightly, moaning to wake up. For a second he thought he had gotten there, because once more he was immobile in the bed, except that his head was hanging down off it, swinging. But he smelled death, and when he opened his eyes he saw the blood-soaked figure of the executioner-priest coming toward him with the stone knife in his hand. He managed to close his eyelids again, although he knew now he was not going to wake up, that he was awake, that the marvelous dream had been the other, absurd as all dreams are—a dream in which he was going through the strange avenues of an astonishing city, with green and red lights that burned without fire or smoke, on an enormous metal insect that whirred away between his legs. In the infinite lie of the dream, they had also picked him up off the ground, someone had approached him also with a knife in his hand, approached him who was lying face up, face up with his eyes closed between the bonfires on the steps.

A M B R O S E   B I E R C E

❧

"AN OCCURRENCE AT OWL
CREEK BRIDGE"

Ambrose Bierce (1842–1914?) was an American journalist,
fiction writer, and poet who lived in San Francisco for much of
his life. While there he became writer-editor of the San Francisco
News Letter and later wrote his famous column "The Prattler."
Three collections of his writing were later published, *In the Midst
of Life, Can Such Things Be,* and *The Devil's Dictionary.* After
breaking with family and friends in 1913, he went to Mexico, where
he disappeared. His imagined fate became the subject of Carlos
Fuentes' novel *The Old Gringo.*

I

      A man stood upon a railroad bridge in
northern Alabama, looking down into the swift water twenty
feet below. The man's hands were behind his back, the wrists
bound with a cord. A rope closely encircled his neck. It was
attached to a stout cross-timber above his head and the slack
fell to the level of his knees. Some loose boards laid upon the
sleepers supporting the metals of the railway supplied a footing for him and his executioners—two private soldiers of the
Federal army, directed by a sergeant who in civil life may have
been a deputy sheriff. At a short remove upon the same temporary platform was an officer in the uniform of his rank,
armed. He was a captain. A sentinel at each end of the bridge
stood with his rifle in the position known as "support," that
is to say, vertical in front of the left shoulder, the hammer
resting on the forearm thrown straight across the chest—

a formal and unnatural position, enforcing an erect carriage of the body. It did not appear to be the duty of these two men to know what was occurring at the centre of the bridge; they merely blockaded the two ends of the foot planking that traversed it.

Beyond one of the sentinels nobody was in sight; the railroad ran straight away into a forest for a hundred yards, then, curving, was lost to view. Doubtless there was an outpost farther along. The other bank of the stream was open ground— a gentle acclivity topped with a stockade of vertical tree trunks, loop-holed for rifles, with a single embrasure through which protruded the muzzle of a brass cannon commanding the bridge. Midway of the slope between bridge and fort were the spectators—a single company of infantry in line, at "parade rest," the butts of the rifles on the ground, the barrels inclining slightly backward against the right shoulder, the hands crossed upon the stock. A lieutenant stood at the right of the line, the point of his sword upon the ground, his left hand resting upon his right. Excepting the group of four at the centre of the bridge, not a man moved. The company faced the bridge, staring stonily, motionless. The sentinels, facing the banks of the stream, might have been statues to adorn the bridge. The captain stood with folded arms, silent, observing the work of his subordinates, but making no sign. Death is a dignitary who when he comes announced is to be received with formal manifestations of respect, even by those most familiar with him. In the code of military etiquette silence and fixity are forms of deference.

The man who was engaged in being hanged was apparently about thirty-five years of age. He was a civilian, if one might judge from his habit, which was that of a planter. His features were good—a straight nose, firm mouth, broad forehead, from which his long, dark hair was combed straight

❧

back, falling behind his ears to the collar of his well-fitting
frock-coat. He wore a mustache and pointed beard, but no
whiskers; his eyes were large and dark gray, and had a kindly
expression which one would hardly have expected in one
whose neck was in the hemp. Evidently this was no vulgar
assassin. The liberal military code makes provision for hanging many kinds of persons, and gentlemen are not excluded.

The preparations being complete, the two private soldiers stepped aside and each drew away the plank upon which
he had been standing. The sergeant turned to the captain,
saluted and placed himself immediately behind that officer,
who in turn moved apart one pace. These movements left the
condemned man and the sergeant standing on the two ends
of the same plank, which spanned three of the cross-ties of
the bridge. The end upon which the civilian stood almost, but
not quite, reached a fourth. This plank had been held in place
by the weight of the captain; it was now held by that of the
sergeant. At a signal from the former the latter would step
aside, the plank would tilt and the condemned man go down
between two ties. The arrangement commended itself to his
judgment as simple and effective. His face had not been covered nor his eyes bandaged. He looked a moment at his
"unsteadfast footing," then let his gaze wander to the swirling
water of the stream racing madly beneath his feet. A piece of
dancing driftwood caught his attention and his eyes followed
it down the current. How slowly it appeared to move! What
a sluggish stream!

He closed his eyes in order to fix his last thoughts upon
his wife and children. The water, touched to gold by the early
sun, the brooding mists under the banks at some distance
down the stream, the fort, the soldiers, the piece of drift—all
had distracted him. And now he became conscious of a new
disturbance. Striking through the thought of his dear ones

was a sound which he could neither ignore nor understand, a sharp, distinct, metallic percussion like the stroke of a blacksmith's hammer upon the anvil; it had the same ringing quality. He wondered what it was, and whether immeasurably distant or near by—it seemed both. Its recurrence was regular, but as slow as the tolling of a death knell. He awaited each stroke with impatience and—he knew not why—apprehension. The intervals of silence grew progressively longer; the delays became maddening. With their greater infrequency the sounds increased in strength and sharpness. They hurt his ear like the thrust of a knife; he feared he would shriek. What he heard was the ticking of his watch.

He unclosed his eyes and saw again the water below him. "If I could free my hands," he thought, "I might throw off the noose and spring into the stream. By diving I could evade the bullets and, swimming vigorously, reach the bank, take to the woods and get away home. My home, thank God, is as yet outside their lines; my wife and little ones are still beyond the invader's farthest advance."

As these thoughts, which have here to be set down in words, were flashed into the doomed man's brain rather than evolved from it the captain nodded to the sergeant. The sergeant stepped aside.

II

Peyton Farquhar was a well-to-do planter, of an old and highly respected Alabama family. Being a slave owner and like other slave owners a politician he was naturally an original secessionist and ardently devoted to the Southern cause. Circumstances of an imperious nature, which it is unnecessary to relate here, had prevented him from taking service with the gallant army that had fought the disastrous campaigns ending with the fall of Corinth, and he chafed under the

〰

inglorious restraint, longing for the release of his energies, the larger life of the soldier, the opportunity for distinction. That opportunity, he felt, would come, as it comes to all in war time. Meanwhile he did what he could. No service was too humble for him to perform in aid of the South, no adventure too perilous for him to undertake if consistent with the character of a civilian who was at heart a soldier, and who in good faith and without too much qualification assented to at least a part of the frankly villainous dictum that all is fair in love and war.

One evening while Farquhar and his wife were sitting on a rustic bench near the entrance to his grounds, a gray-clad soldier rode up to the gate and asked for a drink of water. Mrs. Farquhar was only too happy to serve him with her own white hands. While she was fetching the water her husband approached the dusty horseman and inquired eagerly for news from the front.

"The Yanks are repairing the railroads," said the man, "and are getting ready for another advance. They have reached the Owl Creek bridge, put it in order and built a stockade on the north bank. The commandant has issued an order, which is posted everywhere, declaring that any civilian caught interfering with the railroad, its bridges, tunnels or trains will be summarily hanged. I saw the order."

"How far is it to the Owl Creek bridge?" Farquhar asked.

"About thirty miles."

"Is there no force on this side of the creek?"

"Only a picket post half a mile out, on the railroad, and a single sentinel at this end of the bridge."

"Suppose a man—a civilian and student of hanging—should elude the picket post and perhaps get the better of the sentinel," said Farquhar, smiling, "what could he accomplish?"

The soldier reflected. "I was there a month ago," he replied. "I observed that the flood of last winter had lodged a great quantity of driftwood against the wooden pier at this end of the bridge. It is now dry and would burn like tow."

The lady had now brought the water, which the soldier drank. He thanked her ceremoniously, bowed to her husband and rode away. An hour later, after nightfall, he repassed the plantation, going northward in the direction from which he had come. He was a Federal scout.

III

As Peyton Farquhar fell straight downward through the bridge he lost consciousness and was as one already dead. From this state he was awakened—ages later, it seemed to him—by the pain of a sharp pressure upon his throat, followed by a sense of suffocation. Keen, poignant agonies seemed to shoot from his neck downward through every fibre of his body and limbs. These pains appeared to flash along well-defined lines of ramification and to beat with an inconceivably rapid periodicity. They seemed like streams of pulsating fire heating him to an intolerable temperature. As to his head, he was conscious of nothing but a feeling of fulness—of congestion. These sensations were unaccompanied by thought. The intellectual part of his nature was already effaced; he had power only to feel, and feeling was torment. He was conscious of motion. Encompassed in a luminous cloud, of which he was now merely the fiery heart, without material substance, he swung through unthinkable arcs of oscillation, like a vast pendulum. Then all at once, with terrible suddenness, the light about him shot upward with the noise of a loud plash; a frightful roaring was in his ears, and all was cold and dark. The power of thought was restored; he knew that the rope had broken and he had fallen into the stream. There was no additional strangulation; the noose about his neck was already suffocating him and kept the water from his lungs. To die of hanging at the bottom of a river!—the idea seemed to him ludicrous. He opened his eyes in the darkness and saw above him a gleam of light, but how distant, how inaccessible! He was still sinking, for the light became fainter and fainter until it was a mere glimmer. Then it began to grow and brighten, and he knew that he was rising toward the surface—knew it with reluctance, for he was now very comfortable. "To be hanged and drowned," he thought, "that is not so bad; but I do not wish to be shot. No; I will not be shot; that is not fair."

He was not conscious of an effort, but a sharp pain in his wrist apprised him that he was trying to free his hands. He gave the struggle his attention, as an idler might observe the feat of a juggler, without interest in the outcome. What splendid effort!—what magnificent, what superhuman strength! Ah, that was a fine endeavor! Bravo! The cord fell away; his arms parted and floated upward, the hands dimly seen on each side in the growing light. He watched them with a new interest as first one and then the other pounced upon the noose at his neck. They tore it away and thrust it fiercely aside, its undulations resembling those of a water-snake. "Put it back, put it back!" He thought he shouted these words to his hands, for the undoing of the noose had been succeeded by the direst pang that he had yet experienced. His neck ached horribly; his brain was on fire; his heart, which had been fluttering faintly, gave a great leap, trying to force itself out at his mouth. His whole body was racked and wrenched with an insupportable anguish! But his disobedient hands gave no heed to the command. They beat the water vigorously with quick, downward strokes, forcing him to the surface. He felt his head emerge; his eyes were blinded by the sunlight; his chest expanded convulsively, and with a supreme and crowning agony his lungs engulfed a great draught of air, which instantly he expelled in a shriek!

He was now in full possession of his physical senses. They were, indeed, preternaturally keen and alert. Something in the awful disturbance of his organic system had so exalted and refined them that they made record of things never before perceived. He felt the ripples upon his face and heard their separate sounds as they struck. He looked at the forest on the bank of the stream, saw the individual trees, the leaves and the veining of each leaf—saw the very insects upon them: the locusts, the brilliant-bodied flies, the gray spiders stretching their webs from twig to twig. He noted the prismatic colors in all the dewdrops upon a million blades of grass. The humming of the gnats that danced above the eddies of the stream, the beating of the dragon-flies' wings, the strokes of the water-spiders' legs, like oars which had lifted their boat— all these made audible music. A fish slid along beneath his eyes and he heard the rush of its body parting the water.

He had come to the surface facing down the stream; in a moment the visible world seemed to wheel slowly round, himself the pivotal point, and he saw the bridge, the fort, the soldiers upon the bridge, the captain, the sergeant, the two privates, his executioners. They were in silhouette against the blue sky. They shouted and gesticulated, pointing at him. The captain had drawn his pistol, but did not fire; the others were unarmed. Their movements were grotesque and horrible, their forms gigantic.

Suddenly he heard a sharp report and something struck the water smartly within a few inches of his head, spattering his face with spray. He heard a second report, and saw one of the sentinels with his rifle at his shoulder, a light cloud of blue smoke rising from the muzzle. The man in the water saw the eye of the man on the bridge gazing into his own through the sights of the rifle. He observed that it was a gray eye and remembered having read that gray eyes were keenest, and that all famous marksmen had them. Nevertheless, this one had missed.

A counter-swirl had caught Farquhar and turned him half round; he was again looking into the forest on the bank opposite the fort. The sound of a clear, high voice in a monotonous singsong now rang out behind him and came across the water with a distinctness that pierced and subdued all other sounds, even the beating of the ripples in his ears. Although no soldier, he had frequented camps enough to know the dread significance of that deliberate, drawling, aspirated chant; the lieutenant on shore was taking a part in the morning's work. How coldly and pitilessly—with what an even, calm intonation, presaging, and enforcing tranquillity in the men—with what accurately measured intervals fell those cruel words:

"Attention, company! . . . Shoulder arms! . . . Ready! . . . Aim! . . . Fire!"

Farquhar dived—dived as deeply as he could. The water roared in his ears like the voice of Niagara, yet he heard the dulled thunder of the volley and, rising again toward the surface, met shining bits of metal, singularly flattened, oscillating slowly downward. Some of them touched him on the face and hands, then fell away, continuing their descent. One lodged between his collar and neck; it was uncomfortably warm and he snatched it out.

As he rose to the surface, gasping for breath, he saw that he had been a long time under water; he was perceptibly farther down stream—nearer to safety. The soldiers had almost finished reloading; the metal ramrods flashed all at once in the sunshine as they were drawn from the barrels, turned in the air, and thrust into their sockets. The two sentinels fired again, independently and ineffectually.

The hunted man saw all this over his shoulder; he was now swimming vigorously with the current. His brain was as energetic as his arms and legs; he thought with the rapidity of lightning.

"The officer," he reasoned, "will not make that martinet's error a second time. It is as easy to dodge a volley as a single shot. He has probably already given the command to fire at will. God help me, I cannot dodge them all!"

An appalling plash within two yards of him was followed by a loud, rushing sound, *diminuendo,* which seemed to travel back through the air to the fort and died in an explosion which stirred the very river to its deeps! A rising sheet of water curved over him, fell down upon him, blinded him, strangled him! The cannon had taken a hand in the game. As he shook his head free from the commotion of the smitten water he heard the deflected shot humming through the air ahead, and in an instant it was cracking and smashing the branches in the forest beyond.

"They will not do that again," he thought; "the next time they will use a charge of grape. I must keep my eye upon the gun; the smoke will apprise me—the report arrives too late; it lags behind the missile. That is a good gun."

Suddenly he felt himself whirled round and round—spinning like a top. The water, the banks, the forests, the now distant bridge, fort and men—all were commingled and blurred. Objects were represented by their colors only; circular horizontal streaks of color—that was all he saw. He had been caught in a vortex and was being whirled on with a velocity of advance and gyration that made him giddy and sick. In a few moments he was flung upon the gravel at the

ﺋﻮﺋ

foot of the left bank of the stream—the southern bank—and behind a projecting point which concealed him from his enemies. The sudden arrest of his motion, the abrasion of one of his hands on the gravel, restored him, and he wept with delight. He dug his fingers into the sand, threw it over himself in handfuls and audibly blessed it. It looked like diamonds, rubies, emeralds; he could think of nothing beautiful which it did not resemble. The trees upon the bank were giant garden plants; he noted a definite order in their arrangement, inhaled the fragrance of their blooms. A strange, roseate light shone through the spaces among their trunks and the wind made in their branches the music of æolian harps. He had no wish to perfect his escape—was content to remain in that enchanting spot until retaken.

A whiz and rattle of grapeshot among the branches high above his head roused him from his dream. The baffled cannoneer had fired him a random farewell. He sprang to his feet, rushed up the sloping bank, and plunged into the forest.

All that day he traveled, laying his course by the rounding sun. The forest seemed interminable; nowhere did he discover a break in it, not even a woodman's road. He had not known that he lived in so wild a region. There was something uncanny in the revelation.

By nightfall he was fatigued, footsore, famishing. The thought of his wife and children urged him on. At last he found a road which led him in what he knew to be the right direction. It was as wide and straight as a city street, yet it seemed untraveled. No fields bordered it, no dwelling anywhere. Not so much as the barking of a dog suggested human habitation. The black bodies of the trees formed a straight wall on both sides, terminating on the horizon in a point, like a diagram in a lesson in perspective. Overhead, as he looked up through this rift in the wood, shone great golden stars looking unfamiliar and grouped in strange constellations. He was sure they were arranged in some order which had a secret and malign significance. The wood on either side was full of singular noises, among which—once, twice, and again—he distinctly heard whispers in an unknown tongue.

His neck was in pain and lifting his hand to it he found it horribly swollen. He knew that it had a circle of black where the rope had bruised it. His eyes felt congested; he could no longer close them. His tongue was swollen with thirst; he relieved its fever by thrusting it forward from between his teeth into the cold air. How softly the turf had carpeted the untraveled avenue—he could no longer feel the roadway beneath his feet!

Doubtless, despite his suffering, he had fallen asleep while walking, for now he sees another scene—perhaps he has merely recovered from a delirium. He stands at the gate of his own home. All is as he left it, and all bright and beautiful in the morning sunshine. He must have traveled the entire night. As he pushes open the gate and passes up the wide white walk, he sees a flutter of female garments; his wife, looking fresh and cool and sweet, steps down from the veranda to meet him. At the bottom of the steps she stands waiting, with a smile of ineffable joy, an attitude of matchless grace and dignity. Ah, how beautiful she is! He springs forward with extended arms. As he is about to clasp her he feels a stunning blow upon the back of the neck; a blinding white light blazes all about him with a sound like the shock of a cannon—then all is darkness and silence!

Peyton Farquhar was dead; his body, with a broken neck, swung gently from side to side beneath the timbers of the Owl Creek bridge.

INSPIRATION AND GRATIFICATION

HELEN KELLER

❊

from HELEN KELLER'S JOURNAL: 1936–1937

Helen Keller (1880–1968) is the American memoirist and essayist who was deprived of sight and hearing at the age of nineteen months. She was put in the care of Anne Sullivan, who taught her the relationship between words and objects and became her constant companion. A prolific journal writer, Keller frequently wrote about her dreams. The passage included here was written during her trip through Scotland with Polly Thompson shortly after Sullivan's death in 1936. Thompson, a devoted friend to Keller for over twenty-two years, became a kind of replacement. This dream movingly touches on Keller's relationship with both women, while also revealing the seeds of courage and eternal optimism that shaped this remarkable woman's life.

Central Hotel, Glasgow, December 23rd.

*T*his morning when I awoke my despondency had vanished, and only the sense of a happy dream lingered.

I dreamed that Polly and I landed alone somewhere on the shores of Scotland and got into an automobile. As we started I discovered Teacher seated beside me, glowing with young beauty and joy. We drove through a spring countryside much like South Arcan, Ross Shire, and how she looked and looked! "Oh, Teacher," I cried, "is it not lovely?" "Yes, dear," she answered and kept on gazing. Overjoyed, I knew

✖

her unclouded eyes were taking in the Highland glories of mountain, glen and loch she had not been able to enjoy in her pain and blindness. Sometimes Polly leaned over eagerly to describe the landscape, forgetting Teacher *could see!*

Teacher gave me an instrument covered with soft polished leather and containing coils of wire varying in thickness and sensitivity. "Observe this carefully, Helen," she said, "and it will help you keep your speech at its present level of excellence. It will also bring you different sounds from a distance just as we get them through the ear." I placed my hands on the instrument. To my astonishment each wire coil vibrated with a sound easily distinguishable from the rest— cars and teams going by, passing footsteps, birds singing, running water. I received all these impressions simultaneously, as I do the varied fragrances in a garden of many flowers. Overcome with wonder, I held Teacher's hand. Quietly she drew it back and caressed my cheek, and the next instant I found her place empty, but I was not troubled. I realized the caress was her sign that she had indeed been with me, and it was some time before I waked. Then a luminous peace spread through my heart such as I had not known. I am certain now she *was* there, but I have yet to find out whether the instrument she showed me is an encouragement or a prophecy of new victories over limitations. . . .

JOHN UPDIKE

✇

"DREAM OBJECTS"

John Updike is a prolific and much honored American novelist, short-story writer, and poet. Although best known for his "Rabbit" novels, two of which were the Pulitzer Prize–winning *Rabbit Is Rich* and *Rabbit at Rest,* Updike has also published three volumes of nonfiction prose as well as several volumes of poetry. Updike's writing in both fiction and poetry is characterized by a mild though often irreverent realism. Other novels and short-story collections include *Couples, The Witches of Eastwick, Pigeon Feathers,* and *Trust Me.* His poetry was gathered in *Collected Poems, 1953–1993.*

Strangest is their reality,
their three-dimensional workmanship:
veined pebbles that have an underside,
maps one could have studied for minutes longer,
books we seem to read page after page.

If these are symbols cheaply coined
to buy the mind a momentary pardon,
whence this extravagance? Fine
as dandelion polls, they surface and explode
in the wind of the speed of our dreaming,

❀

so that we awake with the sense
of having missed everything, tourists
hustled by bus through a land whose history
is our rich history, whose artifacts
were filed to perfection by beggars we fear.

❧

from THE   MAGIC   LANTERN:
AN   AUTOBIOGRAPHY

Film audiences have long been familiar with the strikingly intense dream landscapes conjured up in the many films of Swedish film director, scriptwriter, and producer Ingmar Bergman. Bergman's films are usually dark and heavily laden with symbolism; one of his best-known dream sequences is that of the aging professor in the 1957 film *Wild Strawberries* who, on the eve of receiving an honorary degree, dreams of his own corpse reaching out to him from a coffin, and that of the psychologist who, recovering from a recent suicide attempt, dreams that she is attending her own funeral in *Face to Face,* from 1976.

The dream passage here, taken from Bergman's autobiography, *The Magic Lantern,* published in 1988, may come as somewhat of a surprise to viewers of his films. Here he toils with some of the same ideas he touched upon in many of his films, including a preoccupation with aging, but in this case he also reveals an exuberant spirit of confidence and a profound satisfaction for his work.

I am being transported in a large aeroplane and am the only passenger. The plane takes off from the runway but can't gain height, so is roaring along wide streets, keeping at the height of the top floors of the buildings. I can see through the windows, people moving, gesticulating, the day heavy and thundery. I trust the pilot's skill, but realize the end is approaching.

Now I'm floating with no aeroplane, moving my arms in a special way and rising easily from the ground. I am surprised that I have never tried to fly before, when it is so simple. At the same time, I realize this is a special gift, and not everyone can fly. Some who can fly a bit have to strain to the point of exhaustion, their arms bent and the sinews in their necks tense. I float unhindered like a bird.

I find myself above a plain, a steppe presumably. It's bound to be Russia. I float over a huge river and a high bridge. Below the bridge, a brick building protrudes out into the river and clouds of smoke are billowing out of the chimneys. I can hear the roar of machinery. It's a factory.

The river now curves around in a great bend, the banks wooded, the panorama infinite. The sun has gone behind the clouds, but the shadowless light is strong. The water flows along green and transparent in a wide furrow. Sometimes I see shadows moving over stones in the depths and there are huge shimmering fish. I am calm and full of confidence.

When I was younger and slept well, I was tormented by loathsome dreams: murder, torture, suffocation, incest, destruction, insane anger. In my old age, my dreams are escapist, but friendly, often comforting.

Sometimes I dream a brilliant production with great crowds of people, music and colourful sets. I whisper to myself with extreme satisfaction: 'This is my production. I have created this.'

ELIZABETH BISHOP

≈

"SLEEPING STANDING UP"

Elizabeth Bishop (1911–1979), a highly acclaimed American poet, was the recipient of both the Pulitzer Prize and the National Book Award. Known for her stylistic simplicity and subtlety, her frequent writings about her own experiences reflect a sense of irony and detachment. "Sleeping Standing Up" was included in her first volume of poetry, *North and South,* originally published in 1946.

*A*s we lie down to sleep the world turns half away
    through ninety dark degrees;
        the bureau lies on the wall
and thoughts that were recumbent in the day
        rise as the others fall,
    stand up and make a forest of thick-set trees.

The armored cars of dreams, contrived to let us do
    so many a dangerous thing,
        are chugging at its edge
all camouflaged, and ready to go through
        the swiftest streams, or up a ledge
    of crumbling shale, while plates and trappings ring.

—Through turret-slits we saw the crumbs or pebbles that lay
    below the riveted flanks
        on the green forest floor,
like those the clever children placed by day
        and followed to their door
      one night, at least; and in the ugly tanks

we tracked them all the night. Sometimes they disappeared,
    dissolving in the moss,
        sometimes we went too fast
and ground them underneath. How stupidly we steered
      until the night was past
      and never found out where the cottage was.

J. B. PRIESTLEY

※

"DREAMS"

J. B. Priestley (1894–1984), the English novelist, playwright, and essayist, is the author of more than one hundred books. Priestley is best known for his novels, which include *The Good Companions, Angel Pavement,* and *The Image Men,* and for his plays, most notably the internationally acclaimed 1945 play *An Inspector Calls,* which has recently been successfully revived in both London and New York.

*D*reams. Now and again I have had horrible dreams, but not enough of them to make me lose my delight in dreams. To begin with, I like the idea of dreaming, of going to bed and lying still and then, by some queer magic, wandering into another kind of existence. As a child I could never understand why grown-ups took dreaming so calmly when they could make such a fuss about any holiday. This still puzzles me. I am mystified by people who say they never dream and appear to have no interest in the subject. It is much more astonishing than if they said they never went out for a walk. Most people—or at least most Western Europeans—do not seem to accept dreaming as part of their lives. They appear to see it as an irritating little habit, like sneezing or yawning. I have never understood this. My dream life does not seem as important as my waking life, if only because there is far less of it, but to me it *is* important. As if there were at least two extra continents added to the world, and lightning excursions running to them at any moment between midnight and breakfast. Then again, the dream life, though queer and bewildering and unsatisfactory in many respects, has its own advantages. The dead are there, smiling and talking. The past is there, sometimes all broken and confused but occasionally as fresh as a daisy. And perhaps, as Mr. Dunne tells us, the future is there too, winking at us. This dream life is often overshadowed by huge mysterious anxieties, with luggage that cannot be packed and trains that refuse to be caught; and both persons and scenes there are not as dependable and solid as they are in waking life, so that Brown and Smith merge into one person while Robinson splits into two, and there are thick woods outside the bathroom door and the dining room is somehow part of a theater balcony; and there are moments of desolation or terror in the dream world that are worse than anything we have known under the sun. Yet this other life has its interests, its gaieties, its satisfactions, and, at certain rare intervals, a serene glow or a sudden ecstasy, like glimpses of another form of existence altogether, that we cannot match with open eyes. Daft or wise, terrible or exquisite, it is a further helping of experience, a bonus after dark, another slice of life cut differently, for which, it seems to me, we are never sufficiently grateful. Only a dream! Why only? It was there, and you had it. "If there were dreams to sell," Beddoes inquires, "what would you buy?" I cannot say offhand, but certainly rather more than I could afford.

GABRIEL GARCÍA MÁRQUEZ

ⵣ

"I SELL MY DREAMS"

A highly imaginative novelist and short-story writer, Gabriel García Márquez was one of the early South American writers to incorporate magical realism into his work. The Nobel Prize–winning Colombian's acclaimed novels include *One Hundred Years of Solitude, Chronicle of a Death Foretold,* and *Love in the Time of Cholera.* "I Sell Dreams" was published in his short-story collection *Strange Pilgrims.* Set in various European locales, the twelve stories included in this volume were written over a period of eighteen years.

*O*ne morning at nine o'clock, while we were having breakfast on the terrace of the Havana Riviera Hotel under a bright sun, a huge wave picked up several cars that were driving down the avenue along the seawall or parked on the pavement, and embedded one of them in the side of the hotel. It was like an explosion of dynamite that sowed panic on all twenty floors of the building and turned the great entrance window to dust. The many tourists in the lobby were thrown into the air along with the furniture, and some were cut by the hailstorm of glass. The wave must have been immense, because it leaped over the wide two-way street between the seawall and the hotel and still had enough force to shatter the window.

The cheerful Cuban volunteers, with the help of the fire department, picked up the debris in less than six hours, and sealed off the gate to the sea and installed another, and everything returned to normal. During the morning nobody worried about the car encrusted in the wall, for people assumed it was one of those that had been parked on the pavement. But when the crane lifted it out of its setting, the body of a woman was found secured behind the steering wheel by a seat belt. The blow had been so brutal that not a single one of her bones was left whole. Her face was destroyed, her boots had been ripped apart, and her clothes were in shreds. She wore a gold ring shaped like a serpent, with emerald eyes. The police established that she was the housekeeper for the new Portuguese ambassador and his wife. She had come to Havana with them two weeks before and had left that morning for the market, driving a new car. Her name meant nothing to me when I read it in the newspaper, but I was intrigued by the snake ring and its emerald eyes. I could not find out, however, on which finger she wore it.

This was a crucial piece of information, because I feared she was an unforgettable woman whose real name I never knew, and who wore a similar ring on her right forefinger, which in those days was even more unusual than it is now. I had met her thirty-four years earlier in Vienna, eating sausage with boiled potatoes and drinking draft beer in a tavern frequented by Latin American students. I had come from Rome that morning, and I still remember my immediate response to her splendid soprano's bosom, the languid foxtails on her coat collar, and that Egyptian ring in the shape of a serpent. She spoke an elementary Spanish in a metallic accent without pausing for breath, and I thought she was the only Austrian at the long wooden table. But no, she had been born in Colombia and had come to Austria between the wars, when she was little more than a child, to study music and voice. She was about thirty, and did not carry her years well, for she had never been pretty and had begun to age before her time. But she was a charming human being. And one of the most awe-inspiring.

Vienna was still an old imperial city, whose geographical position between the two irreconcilable worlds left behind by the Second World War had turned it into a paradise of black marketeering and international espionage. I could not have imagined a more suitable spot for my fugitive compatriot, who still ate in the students' tavern on the corner only out of loyalty to her origins, since she had more than enough money to buy meals for all her table companions. She never told her real name, and we always knew her by the Germanic tongue twister that we Latin American students in Vienna invented for her: Frau Frieda. I had just been introduced to her when I committed the happy impertinence of asking how she had come to be in a world so distant and different from the windy cliffs of Quindío, and she answered with a devastating:

"I sell my dreams."

In reality, that was her only trade. She had been the third of eleven children born to a prosperous shopkeeper in old Caldas, and as soon as she learned to speak she instituted the fine custom in her family of telling dreams before breakfast, the time when their oracular qualities are preserved in their purest form. When she was seven she dreamed that one of her brothers was carried off by a flood. Her mother, out of sheer religious superstition, forbade the boy to swim in the ravine, which was his favorite pastime. But Frau Frieda already had her own system of prophecy.

"What that dream means," she said, "isn't that he's going to drown, but that he shouldn't eat sweets."

Her interpretation seemed an infamy to a five-year-old boy who could not live without his Sunday treats. Their mother, convinced of her daughter's oracular talents, enforced the warning with an iron hand. But in her first careless moment the boy choked on a piece of caramel that he was eating in secret, and there was no way to save him.

Frau Frieda did not think she could earn a living with her talent until life caught her by the throat during the cruel Viennese winters. Then she looked for work at the first house where she would have liked to live, and when she was asked what she could do, she told only the truth: "I dream." A brief explanation to the lady of the house was all she needed, and she was hired at a salary that just covered her minor expenses, but she had a nice room and three meals a day—breakfast in particular, when the family sat down to learn the immediate future of each of its members: the father, a refined financier; the mother, a joyful woman passionate about Romantic chamber music; and two children, eleven and nine years old. They were all religious and therefore inclined to archaic superstitions, and they were delighted to take in Frau Frieda, whose only obligation was to decipher the family's daily fate through her dreams.

She did her job well, and for a long time, above all during the war years, when reality was more sinister than nightmares. Only she could decide at breakfast what each should do that day, and how it should be done, until her predictions became the sole authority in the house. Her control over the family was absolute: Even the faintest sigh was breathed by her order. The master of the house died at about the time I was in Vienna, and had the elegance to leave her a part of his estate on the condition that she continue dreaming for the family until her dreams came to an end.

I stayed in Vienna for more than a month, sharing the straitened circumstances of the other students while I waited for money that never arrived. Frau Frieda's unexpected and generous visits to the tavern were like fiestas in our poverty-stricken regime. One night, in a beery euphoria, she whispered in my ear with a conviction that permitted no delay.

"I only came to tell you that I dreamed about you last night," she said. "You must leave right away and not come back to Vienna for five years."

Her conviction was so real that I boarded the last train to Rome that same night. As for me, I was so influenced by what she said that from then on I considered myself a survivor of some catastrophe I never experienced. I still have not returned to Vienna.

Before the disaster in Havana, I had seen Frau Frieda in Barcelona in so unexpected and fortuitous a way that it seemed a mystery to me. It happened on the day Pablo Neruda stepped on Spanish soil for the first time since the Civil War, on a stopover during a long sea voyage to Valparaíso. He spent a morning with us hunting big game in the secondhand bookstores, and at Porter he bought an old, dried-out volume with a torn binding for which he paid what would have been his salary for two months at the consulate in Rangoon. He moved through the crowd like an invalid elephant, with a child's curiosity in the inner workings of each thing he saw, for the world appeared to him as an immense wind-up toy with which life invented itself.

I have never known anyone closer to the idea one has of a Renaissance pope: He was gluttonous and refined. Even against his will, he always presided at the table. Matilde, his wife, would put a bib around his neck that belonged in a barbershop rather than a dining room, but it was the only way to keep him from taking a bath in sauce. That day at Carvalleiras was typical. He ate three whole lobsters, dissecting them with a surgeon's skill, and at the same time devoured everyone else's plate with his eyes and tasted a little from each with a delight that made the desire to eat contagious: clams from Galicia, mussels from Cantabria, prawns from Alicante, sea cucumbers from the Costa Brava. In the meantime, like the French, he spoke of nothing but other culinary delicacies, in particular the prehistoric shellfish of Chile, which he carried in his heart. All at once he stopped eating, tuned his lobster's antennae, and said to me in a very quiet voice:

"There's someone behind me who won't stop looking at me."

I glanced over his shoulder, and it was true. Three tables away sat an intrepid woman in an old-fashioned felt hat and a purple scarf, eating without haste and staring at him. I recognized her right away. She had grown old and fat, but it was Frau Frieda, with the snake ring on her index finger.

She was traveling from Naples on the same ship as Neruda and his wife, but they had not seen each other on board. We invited her to have coffee at our table, and I encouraged her to talk about her dreams in order to astound the poet. He paid no attention, for from the very beginning he had announced that he did not believe in prophetic dreams.

"Only poetry is clairvoyant," he said.

After lunch, during the inevitable stroll along the Ramblas, I lagged behind with Frau Frieda so that we could renew our memories with no other ears listening. She told me she had sold her properties in Austria and retired to Oporto, in Portugal, where she lived in a house that she described as a fake castle on a hill, from which one could see all the way across the ocean to the Americas. Although she did not say so, her conversation made it clear that, dream by dream, she had taken over the entire fortune of her ineffable patrons in

Vienna. That did not surprise me, however, because I had always thought her dreams were no more than a stratagem for surviving. And I told her so.

She laughed her irresistible laugh. "You're as impudent as ever," she said. And said no more, because the rest of the group had stopped to wait for Neruda to finish talking in Chilean slang to the parrots along the Rambla de los Pájaros. When we resumed our conversation, Frau Frieda changed the subject.

"By the way," she said, "you can go back to Vienna now."

Only then did I realize that thirteen years had gone by since our first meeting.

"Even if your dreams are false, I'll never go back," I told her. "Just in case."

At three o'clock we left her to accompany Neruda to his sacred siesta, which he took in our house after solemn preparations that in some way recalled the Japanese tea ceremony. Some windows had to be opened and others closed to achieve the perfect degree of warmth, and there had to be a certain kind of light from a certain direction, and absolute silence. Neruda fell asleep right away, and woke ten minutes later, as children do, when we least expected it. He appeared in the living room refreshed, and with the monogram of the pillowcase imprinted on his cheek.

"I dreamed about that woman who dreams," he said.

Matilde wanted him to tell her his dream.

"I dreamed she was dreaming about me," he said.

"That's right out of Borges," I said.

He looked at me in disappointment.

"Has he written it already?"

"If he hasn't he'll write it sometime," I said. "It will be one of his labyrinths."

As soon as he boarded the ship at six that evening, Neruda took his leave of us, sat down at an isolated table, and began to write fluid verses in the green ink he used for drawing flowers and fish and birds when he dedicated his books. At the first "All ashore" we looked for Frau Frieda, and found her at last on the tourist deck, just as we were about to leave without saying good-bye. She too had taken a siesta.

"I dreamed about the poet," she said.

In astonishment I asked her to tell me her dream.

"I dreamed he was dreaming about me," she said, and my look of amazement disconcerted her. "What did you expect? Sometimes, with all my dreams, one slips in that has nothing to do with real life."

I never saw her again or even wondered about her until I heard about the snake ring on the woman who died in the Havana Riviera disaster. And I could not resist the temptation of questioning the Portuguese ambassador when we happened to meet some months later at a diplomatic reception. The ambassador spoke about her with great enthusiasm and enormous admiration. "You cannot imagine how extraordinary she was," he said. "You would have been obliged to write a story about her." And he went on in the same tone, with surprising details, but without the clue that would have allowed me to come to a final conclusion.

"In concrete terms," I asked at last, "what did she do?"

"Nothing," he said, with a certain disenchantment. "She dreamed."

March 1980

JORGE   LUIS   BORGES

❧

"THE   CIRCULAR   RUINS"

Argentinean Jorge Luis Borges (1899–1986) was a prolific author of
essays, poetry, and short fiction. His carefully wrought approach to
the metaphysical preoccupations of mankind was a major influence
on many contemporary Latin American writers. His writing is often
a blend of myth, fantasy, and symbolism; and his signature image,
of life as a type of labyrinth through which one passes, is central to
this representative Borges story, "The Circular Ruins."

And if he left off dreaming about you . . .
—*Through the Looking Glass,* VI.

*N*o one saw him disembark in the unan-
imous night, no one saw the bamboo canoe sink into the
sacred mud, but in a few days there was no one who did not
know that the taciturn man came from the South and that his
home had been one of those numberless villages upstream
in the deeply cleft side of the mountain, where the Zend
language has not been contaminated by Greek and where
leprosy is infrequent. What is certain is that the gray man
kissed the mud, climbed up the bank without pushing aside
(probably, without feeling) the blades which were lacerating
his flesh, and crawled, nauseated and bloodstained, up to the
circular enclosure crowned with a stone tiger or horse, which
sometimes was the color of flame and now was that of ashes.
This circle was a temple which had been devoured by ancient
fires, profaned by the miasmal jungle, and whose god no

❁

longer received the homage of men. The stranger stretched himself out beneath the pedestal. He was awakened by the sun high overhead. He was not astonished to find that his wounds had healed; he closed his pallid eyes and slept, not through weakness of flesh but through determination of will. He knew that this temple was the place required for his invincible intent; he knew that the incessant trees had not succeeded in strangling the ruins of another propitious temple downstream which had once belonged to gods now burned and dead; he knew that his immediate obligation was to dream. Toward midnight he was awakened by the inconsolable shriek of a bird. Tracks of bare feet, some figs and a jug warned him that the men of the region had been spying respectfully on his sleep, soliciting his protection or afraid of his magic. He felt a chill of fear, and sought out a sepulchral niche in the dilapidated wall where he concealed himself among unfamiliar leaves.

The purpose which guided him was not impossible, though supernatural. He wanted to dream a man; he wanted to dream him in minute entirety and impose him on reality. This magic project had exhausted the entire expanse of his mind; if some one had asked him his name or to relate some event of his former life, he would not have been able to give an answer. This uninhabited, ruined temple suited him, for it contained a minimum of visible world; the proximity of the workmen also suited him, for they took it upon themselves to provide for his frugal needs. The rice and fruit they brought him were nourishment enough for his body, which was consecrated to the sole task of sleeping and dreaming.

At first, his dreams were chaotic; then in a short while they became dialectic in nature. The stranger dreamed that he was in the center of a circular amphitheater which was more or less the burnt temple; clouds of taciturn students filled the tiers of seats; the faces of the farthest ones hung at a distance of many centuries and as high as the stars, but their features were completely precise. The man lectured his pupils on anatomy, cosmography, and magic: the faces listened anxiously and tried to answer understandingly, as if they guessed the importance of that examination which would redeem one of them from his condition of empty illusion and interpolate him into the real world. Asleep or awake, the man thought over the answers of his phantoms, did not allow himself to be deceived by imposters, and in certain perplexities he sensed a growing intelligence. He was seeking a soul worthy of participating in the universe.

After nine or ten nights he understood with a certain bitterness that he could expect nothing from those pupils who accepted his doctrine passively, but that he could expect something from those who occasionally dared to oppose him. The former group, although worthy of love and affection, could not ascend to the level of individuals; the latter pre-existed to a slightly greater degree. One afternoon (now afternoons were also given over to sleep, now he was only awake for a couple of hours at daybreak) he dismissed the vast illusory student body for good and kept only one pupil. He was a taciturn, sallow boy, at times intractable, and whose sharp features resembled those of his dreamer. The brusque elimination of his fellow students did not disconcert him for long; after a few private lessons, his progress was enough to astound the teacher. Nevertheless, a catastrophe took place. One day, the man emerged from his sleep as if from a viscous desert, looked at the useless afternoon light which he immediately confused with the dawn, and understood that he had not dreamed. All that night and all day long, the intolerable lucidity of insomnia fell upon him. He tried exploring the forest, to lose his strength; among the hemlock he barely succeeded in experiencing several short snatches of sleep, veined with fleeting, rudimentary visions that were useless. He tried to assemble the student body but scarcely had he articulated a few brief words of exhortation when it became deformed and was then erased. In his almost perpetual vigil, tears of anger burned his old eyes.

He understood that modeling the incoherent and vertiginous matter of which dreams are composed was the most difficult task that a man could undertake, even though he should penetrate all the enigmas of a superior and inferior order; much more difficult than weaving a rope out of sand or coining the faceless wind. He swore he would forget the enormous hallucination which had thrown him off at first, and he sought another method of work. Before putting it into execution, he spent a month recovering his strength, which had been squandered by his delirium. He abandoned all premeditation of dreaming and almost immediately succeeded in sleeping a reasonable part of each day. The few times that he had dreams during this period, he paid no attention to them. Before resuming his task, he waited until the moon's disk was perfect. Then, in the afternoon, he purified himself in the waters of the river, worshipped the planetary gods, pronounced the prescribed syllables of a mighty name, and went to sleep. He dreamed almost immediately, with his heart throbbing.

He dreamed that it was warm, secret, about the size of a clenched fist, and of a garnet color within the penumbra of a human body as yet without face or sex; during fourteen lucid nights he dreamt of it with meticulous love. Every night he perceived it more clearly. He did not touch it; he only permitted himself to witness it, to observe it, and occasionally to rectify it with a glance. He perceived it and lived it from all angles and distances. On the fourteenth night he lightly touched the pulmonary artery with his index finger, then the whole heart, outside and inside. He was satisfied with the examination. He deliberately did not dream for a night; he then took up the heart again, invoked the name of a planet, and undertook the vision of another of the principle organs. Within a year he had come to the skeleton and the eyelids. The innumerable hair was perhaps the most difficult task. He dreamed an entire man—a young man, but who did not sit up or talk, who was unable to open his eyes. Night after night, the man dreamt him asleep.

In the Gnostic cosmogonies, demiurges fashion a red Adam who cannot stand; as clumsy, crude and elemental as this Adam of dust was the Adam of dreams forged by the wizard's nights. One afternoon, the man almost destroyed his entire work, but then changed his mind. (It would have been better had he destroyed it.) When he had exhausted all supplications to the deities of the earth, he threw himself at the feet of the effigy which was perhaps a tiger or perhaps a colt and implored its unknown help. That evening, at twilight, he dreamt of the statue. He dreamt it was alive, tremulous: it was not an atrocious bastard of a tiger and a colt, but at the same time those two fiery creatures and also a bull, a rose, and a storm. This multiple god revealed to him that his earthly name was Fire, and that in this circular temple (and in others like it) people had once made sacrifices to him and worshipped him, and that he would magically animate the dreamed phantom, in such a way that all creatures, except Fire itself and the dreamer, would believe it to be a man of flesh and blood. He commanded that once this man had been instructed in all the rites, he should be sent to the other ruined temple whose pyramids were still standing downstream, so that some voice would glorify him in that deserted edifice. In the dream of the man that dreamed, the dreamed one awoke.

❈

The wizard carried out the orders he had been given. He devoted a certain length of time (which finally proved to be two years) to instructing him in the mysteries of the universe and the cult of fire. Secretly, he was pained at the idea of being separated from him. On the pretext of pedagogical necessity, each day he increased the number of hours dedicated to dreaming. He also remade the right shoulder, which was somewhat defective. At times, he was disturbed by the impression that all this had already happened. . . . In general, his days were happy; when he closed his eyes, he thought: *Now I will be with my son.* Or, more rarely: *The son I have engendered is waiting for me and will not exist if I do not go to him.*

Gradually, he began accustoming him to reality. Once he ordered him to place a flag on a faraway peak. The next day the flag was fluttering on the peak. He tried other analogous experiments, each time more audacious. With a certain bitterness, he understood that his son was ready to be born— and perhaps impatient. That night he kissed him for the first time and sent him off to the other temple whose remains were turning white downstream, across many miles of inextricable jungle and marshes. Before doing this (and so that his son should never know that he was a phantom, so that he should think himself a man like any other) he destroyed in him all memory of his years of apprenticeship.

His victory and peace became blurred with boredom. In the twilight times of dusk and dawn, he would prostrate himself before the stone figure, perhaps imagining his unreal son carrying out identical rites in other circular ruins downstream; at night he no longer dreamed, or dreamed as any man does. His perceptions of the sounds and forms of the universe became somewhat pallid; his absent son was being nourished by these diminutions of his soul. The purpose of his life had been fulfilled; the man remained in a kind of ecstasy. After a certain time, which some chroniclers prefer to compute in years and others in decades, two oarsmen awoke him at midnight; he could not see their faces, but they spoke to him of a charmed man in a temple of the North, capable of walking on fire without burning himself. The wizard suddenly remembered the words of the god. He remembered that of all the creatures that people the earth, Fire was the only one who knew his son to be a phantom. This memory, which at first calmed him, ended by tormenting him. He feared lest his son should meditate on this abnormal privilege and by some means find out he was a mere simulacrum. Not to be a man, to be a projection of another man's dreams—what an incomparable humiliation, what madness! Any father is interested in the sons he has procreated (or permitted) out of the mere confusion of happiness; it was natural that the wizard should fear for the future of that son whom he had thought out entrail by entrail, feature by feature, in a thousand and one secret nights.

His misgivings ended abruptly, but not without certain forewarnings. First (after a long drought) a remote cloud, as light as a bird, appeared on a hill; then, toward the South, the sky took on the rose color of leopard's gums; then came clouds of smoke which rusted the metal of the nights; afterwards came the panic-stricken flight of wild animals. For what had happened many centuries before was repeating itself. The ruins of the sanctuary of the god of Fire was destroyed by fire. In a dawn without birds, the wizard saw the concentric fire licking the walls. For a moment, he thought of taking refuge in the water, but then he understood that death was coming to crown his old age and absolve him from his labors. He walked toward the sheets of flame.

❀

They did not bite his flesh, they caressed him and flooded him without heat or combustion. With relief, with humiliation, with terror, he understood that he also was an illusion, that someone else was dreaming him.

SOURCES

❧ ATWOOD, MARGARET From *Lady Oracle* by Margaret Atwood. Copyright © 1976 by Margaret Atwood. Reprinted by permission of Simon & Schuster and McClelland & Stewart, Inc. ❧ BARKER, PAT From *Regeneration* by Pat Barker. Copyright © 1991 by Pat Barker. Used by permission of Dutton Signet, a division of Penguin Books USA Inc. ❧ BARTHELME, DONALD "A Few Moments of Sleeping and Waking" from *Forty Stories* by Donald Barthelme. Copyright © 1987 by Donald Barthelme. Reprinted by permission of The Putnam Publishing Group and The Wylie Agency, Inc. ❧ BERGMAN, INGMAR From *The Magic Lantern* by Ingmar Bergman, translated by Joan Tate, translation copyright © 1988 by Joan Tate. Original copyright © 1987 by Ingmar Bergman. Used by permission of Viking Penguin, a division of Penguin Books USA Inc. ❧ BISHOP, ELIZABETH "Sleeping Standing Up" from *The Complete Poems 1927–1979* by Elizabeth Bishop. Copyright © 1979, 1983 by Alice Helen Methfessel. Reprinted by permission of Farrar, Straus & Giroux. ❧ BORGES, JORGE LUIS "The Circular Ruins" from *Ficciones* by Jorge Luis Borges, translated by Anthony Bonner, copyright © 1962 by Grove Press, Inc. Used by permission of Grove/Atlantic, Inc., and Weidenfeld & Nicolson. ❧ CHEEVER, JOHN From *The Journals of John Cheever*, copyright © 1990, 1991 by Mary Cheever, Susan Cheever, Benjamin Cheever, and Federico Cheever. Reprinted by permission of Alfred A. Knopf, Inc. ❧ COCTEAU, JEAN "On Dreams" from *The Difficulty of Being* by Jean Cocteau. Copyright © 1957 by Editions du Rocher Monaco. English translation copyright © 1966 by Elizabeth Sprigge. Reprinted by permission of Peter Owen Limited, London. ❧ CORTÁZAR, JULIO "The Night Face Up" from *End of the Game and Other Stories* by Julio Cortázar, translated by Paul Blackburn. Copyright © 1967 by

Weinberger. Reprinted by permission of New Directions
Publishing Corp. ✑ PORTER, KATHERINE ANNE From
"Pale Horse, Pale Rider" in *Pale Horse, Pale Rider: Three Short
Novels*, copyright 1937 and renewed 1965 by Katherine Anne
Porter, reprinted by permission of Harcourt Brace & Company.
✑ PRICE, REYNOLDS "Washed Feet" from *The Collected
Stories* by Reynolds Price. Copyright © 1993 by Reynolds Price.
Reprinted by permission of Scribner, a division of Simon &
Schuster. ✑ PRIESTLEY, J. B. "Dreams" from *Delight* by J.
B. Priestley. Copyright © 1949 by J. B. Priestley. Reprinted by
permission of The Peters Fraser & Dunlop Group Limited. ✑
ROETHKE, THEODORE "The Dream" from *The Collected
Poems of Theodore Roethke* by Theodore Roethke. Copyright ©
1955 by Theodore Roethke. Used by permission of Doubleday, a
division of Bantam Doubleday Dell Publishing Group, Inc. ✑
ROTH, PHILIP From *Portnoy's Complaint* by Philip Roth.
Copyright © 1969 by Philip Roth. Reprinted by permission of
Random House, Inc. ✑ THOMAS, D. M. From *The White
Hotel* by D. M. Thomas. Copyright © 1981 by D. M. Thomas.
Used by permission of Viking Penguin, a division of Penguin
Books USA Inc., and John Johnson, Ltd. ✑ TREVOR,
WILLIAM From *Felicia's Journey* by William Trevor. Copyright
© 1994 by William Trevor. Used by permission of Viking Penguin,
a division of Penguin Books USA Inc. ✑ UPDIKE, JOHN
"Dream Objects," from *Collected Poems 1953–1993* by John
Updike. Copyright © 1993 by John Updike. Reprinted by
permission of Alfred A. Knopf, Inc. ✑ WIDEMAN, JOHN
EDGAR Excerpt from *Fever: Twelve Stories* by John Edgar
Wideman. Copyright © 1981 by John Edgar Wideman. Reprinted
by permission of Henry Holt & Co., Inc. ✑ WILSON,
EDMUND Excerpts from *The Fifties* by Edmund Wilson.
Copyright © 1986 by Helen Miranda Wilson. Excerpts from *The
Forties* by Edmund Wilson. Copyright © 1983 by Helen Miranda

Donald Barthelme   STANLEY ELKIN   Jean Cocteau
Roethke   D. M. Thomas   Sigmund Freud   ARCHIBALD M
OCTAVIO PAZ   Katherine Mansfield   Edmund Wi
Naipaul   Doris Lessing   C. G. JUNG   Pat Barker   M.
Didion   Graham Greene   C. S. Lewis   SHOLOM
Porter   VIRGINIA WOOLF   James Hillman   John Edgar
John Updike   Ingmar Bergman   ELIZABETH BISH
DONALD BARTHELME   Stanley Elkin   Jean Cocteau   Alle
D. M. Thomas   SIGMUND FREUD   Archibald
Octavio Paz   Katherine Mansfield   Edmund Wilson   PH
DORIS LESSING   C. G. Jung   Pat Barker   M. F. K. Fisher
Graham Greene   C. S. LEWIS   Sholom Aleichem
Virginia Woolf   James Hillman   John Edgar Wideman   J
Ingmar Bergman   Elizabeth Bishop   J. B. PRIESTLEY
Barthelme   STANLEY ELKIN   Jean Cocteau   Allen Ginsberg
Thomas   Sigmund Freud   ARCHIBALD MACLEISH   Edn
Katherine Mansfield   Edmund Wilson   Philip Larkin
Lessing   C. G. JUNG   Pat Barker   M. F. K. Fisher
Greene   C. S. Lewis   SHOLOM ALEICHEM   Margaret A
James Hillman   John Edgar Wideman   Julio Cortáz
Bergman   ELIZABETH BISHOP   J. B. Priestley
Stanley Elkin   Jean Cocteau   Allen Ginsberg   PHILIP
SIGMUND FREUD   Archibald MacLeish   Edna O'Brien
Katherine Mansfield   Edmund Wilson   PHILIP LARKIN
LESSING   C. G. Jung   Pat Barker   M. F. K. Fishe
Greene   C. S. LEWIS   Sholom Aleichem   Margaret
Woolf   James Hillman   John Edgar Wideman   Julio
Ingmar Bergman   Elizabeth Bishop   J. B. PRIESTLEY
STANLEY ELKIN   Jean Cocteau   Allen Ginsberg   Philip
Thomas   Sigmund Freud   ARCHIBALD MACLEISH   Ed
Katherine Mansfield   Edmund Wilson   Philip Larkin
Lessing   C. G. JUNG   Pat Barker   M. F. K. Fisher   Fyo
Greene   C. S. Lewis   SHOLOM ALEICHEM   Margaret A
James Hillman   John Edgar Wideman   Julio
Ingmar Bergman   ELIZABETH BISHOP   J. B. Priestley
Stanley Elkin   Jean Cocteau   Allen Ginsberg   PHIL
SIGMUND FREUD   Archibald MacLeish   Edna O'Bri